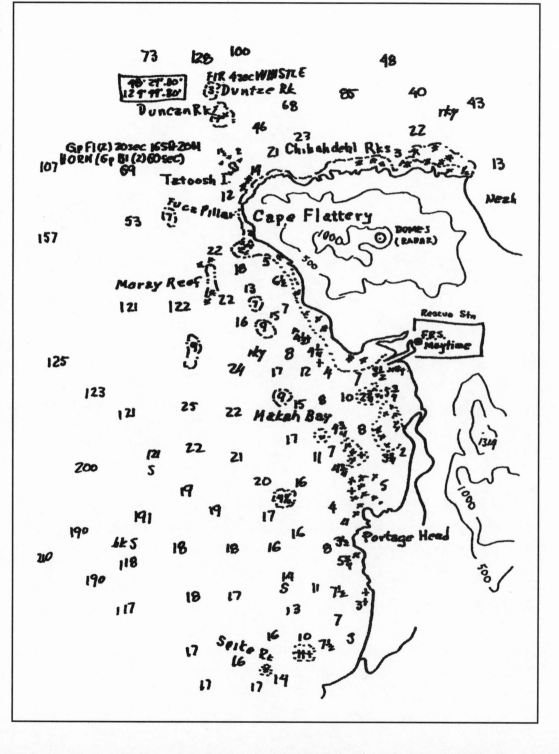

RICHARD BACH

THE FERRET CHRONICLES

Illustrated by the Author

Ferret House Press

RESCUE
FERRETS
AT SEA

RESCUE

RESOLUTE

SCRIBNER

NEW YORK   LONDON   TORONTO   SYDNEY   SINGAPORE

SCRIBNER
1230 Avenue of the Americas
New York, NY 10020

SCRIBNER and design are trademarks of Macmillan Library
Reference USA, Inc., used under license by Simon & Schuster,
the publisher of this work.

For information regarding special discounts for bulk purchases,
please contact Simon & Schuster Special Sales at 1-800-456-6798
or business@simonandschuster.com

Designed by Carla J. Stanley

Text set in Frys Baskerville

Manufactured in the United States of America

1   3   5   7   9   10   8   6   4   2

Library of Congress Cataloging-in-Publication Data
Bach, Richard.
Rescue ferrets at sea/Richard Bach.
p. cm.—(The ferret chronicles)
1. Ferrets—Fiction. I. Title.
PS3552.A255 R47 2002
813'.54—dc21
2002017620

ISBN 0-7432-2750-6

RESCUE FERRETS AT SEA

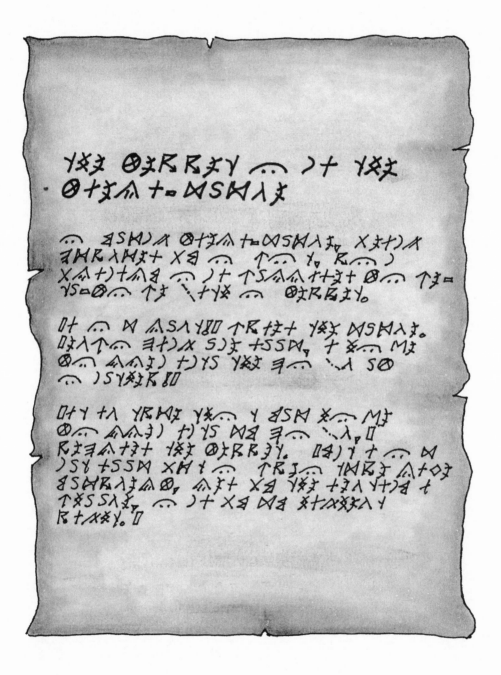

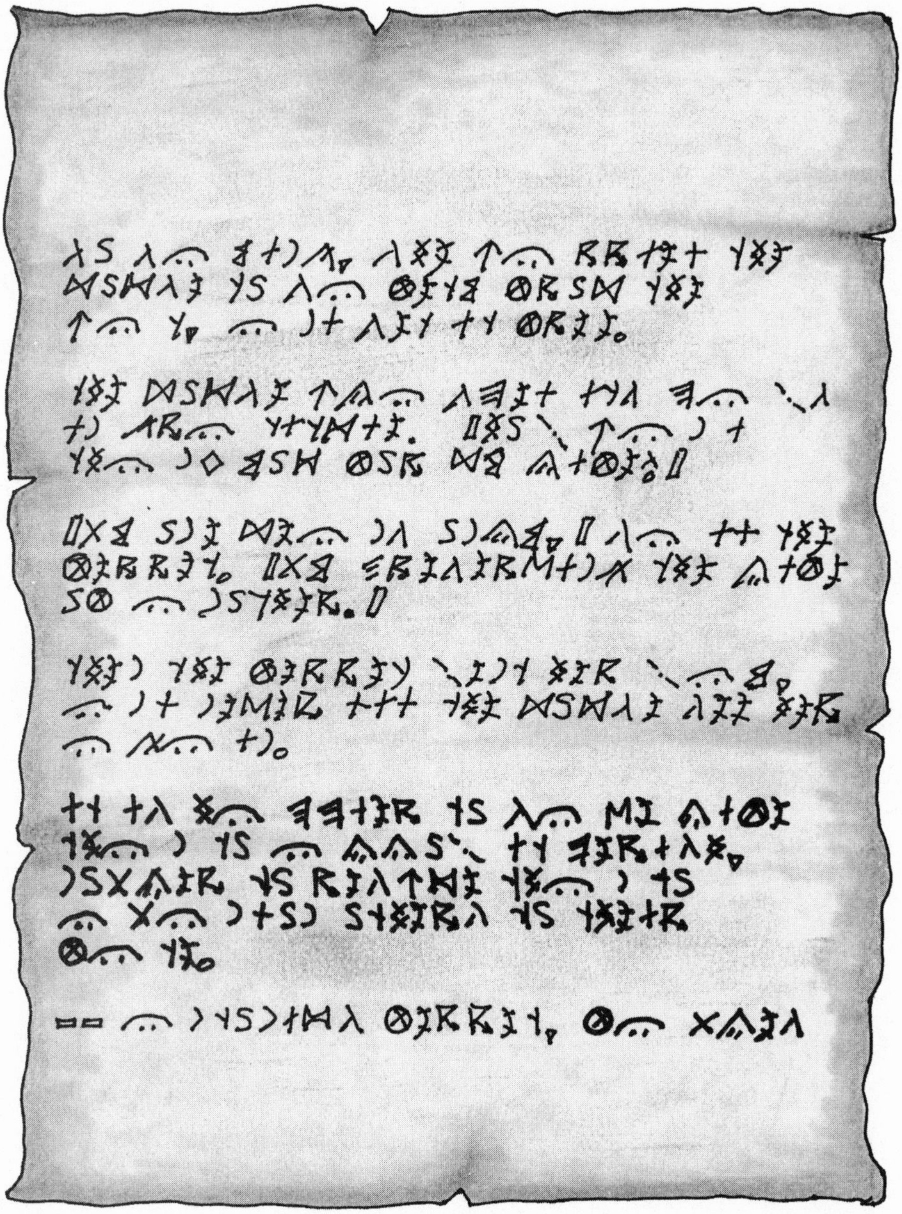

The Ferret and the Field-Mouse

A young field-mouse, being pursued by a cat, ran blindly and collided face-to-face with a ferret.

"I am lost!" cried the mouse. "Escaping one doom, I have fallen into the paws of another!"

"It is true that you have fallen into my paws," replied the ferret. "Yet I am not doom but a creature like yourself, led by the destiny I choose, and by my highest right."

So saying, she carried the mouse to safety from the cat and set it free.

The mouse clasped its paws in gratitude. "How can I thank you for my life?"

"By one means only," said the ferret. "By preserving the life of another."

Then the ferret went her way, and never did the mouse see her again.

It is happier to save life than to allow it perish, nobler to rescue from distress than to abandon others to their fate.

—Antonius Ferret, *Fables*

CHAPTER 1

Stars turning ever so slowly above a cool summer dark, Katrinka Ferret lifted her two kits, sister and little brother, and set them softly down in their hammock for the night. Walls of stone released the heat of the day into the ferrets' home, and the kits, freshly bathed, waited for their bedtime story.

Katrinka slid her paw slowly along the row of books on their bedroom shelf, her eyes on the little ones waiting for the right instant.

"That one!" cried Bethany and Vincent together, and in that moment their mother stayed her paw and pulled forth the volume that it touched. She knew the book by feel, by the worn, bent corners of the cover.

Still watching her kits, before even glancing at the title she opened her eyes wide in mock surprise.

"My goodness, what have we here?" said she. "Is this by any chance called *Rescue Ferrets at Sea*?"

So often had she held the book and read the story that it was long memorized, but the two cried, "Yes! Yes!" as though she had magically plucked the volume from empty space.

"Then settle down, my kits," she said, "and I shall tell you the story of the little ferrets who went to sea. . . ."

Bethany Nikka, the eldest, snuggled into her favorite spot in the hammock, chin on the edge of the warm fluff, nose and whiskers pointed in rapt attention to her mother. Eyes already closed, she fell deep into imagination, waiting.

Vincent lay alongside, one paw holding his stuffed hedgehog, rustling himself into the most comfortable position that the remaining hammock would allow. Someday, he knew, it would be his hammock alone. Tonight he was happy to be with his sister, he wanted her to have the best spot for herself.

"'Once upon a time,'" their mother began, "'by the edge of a great ocean, there was a party of kits, out for a romp. Adventurous they were, but not very wise, for they determined to sail from the land to the Forbidden Island offshore. . . .'"

Here she opened the book to show the picture of the adventurous-but-not-very-wise youngsters, clustering about a driftwood raft and bedsheet sail. Bethany nodded, eyes closed, for she saw the picture in her mind.

Oh, those foolish kits! she thought, for she knew that even as they left the shore a monstrous bubble-storm was frothing toward Forbidden Island, unseen and unknown to the voyagers.

She saw it while her mother read: the all-day sail to the island, the carefree ferrets swept there more by current than skill, she saw them tumbling ashore, exploring with no thought for night approaching, ignorant of a sky signaling the storm ahead. She saw the flash, she heard the crack of thunder. The foolish kits were trapped.

"What shall we do?" she whispered, barely moving her lips.

"'*What shall we do?*'" Katrinka read, holding up the picture, two pages wide, the six hapless ferrets stranded on a speck of land, surrounded by a wall of bubbles.

"What could be done?" both kits said, with their mother.

Bethany saw it all as it happened: the storm advancing ruthlessly; the great ships racing to port to escape the fury of an ocean gone wild; the poor kits clinging like furry flags to tree trunks before they were blown head over heels to the ground; the discovery by parents that their little ones were missing, with barely a bag of ferret food to sustain them; the storm raging on. At last the wind subsiding but the island and the sea about it smothered deep in bubbles, no way for land creatures to sail.

"'What could be done?'" their mother read.

"CALL THE RESCUE FERRETS!" cried the kits together.

"Exactly right," Katrinka said. *"Call the rescue ferrets!"* She turned the page.

Bethany watched the story unfold so clearly that she nearly stopped breathing. The clangor of the alarm bell on the dock of the Ferret Rescue Station, Captain Terry Ferret and his Alert Crew dashing to their posts, the low-thunder roar of twin engines lighting off, lines casting away a-splash in the wake of the sleek vessel setting forth on a mission of mercy.

Out from the channel came the rescue animals, the mass of bubbles parting ahead, flying aside as the bubble-breaker *Emily T. Ferret* sliced on a course to Forbidden Island.

So brave! Bethany thought as she pictured Captain Terry, though she knew he was too busy to acknowledge admiration.

He steered by dead reckoning, daring a straight-line compass course through the shipping lanes for the island, both engines at full throttle, his boat at flank speed, as fast as it could go. He watched his radar for returns from ships in his path, but the bubbles blurred the electric picture. More than radar he trusted the keen ears of his crew listening for echoes ahead to avoid a collision that would send them all to the bottom.

Meanwhile, the kits on the island, engulfed in bubbles, were holding paws so as not to be lost one from the other. They finished their rations, sharing their ferret food to the final crumb. They huddled close, shivering with cold, doubting they would live to see tomorrow's sunset. How foolish they had been to take such a trip for a lark, and how sorry they were now for having done so!

"Ship ahead, Captain!"

Bethany saw what Captain Terry Ferret saw, the sudden-looming radar blur of a human's freighter, come to a dead stop in the sea, blocking the way ahead.

"Right full rudder!" he cried to his helmsferret and the rescue boat careened wildly at top speed, spray and bubbles flying.

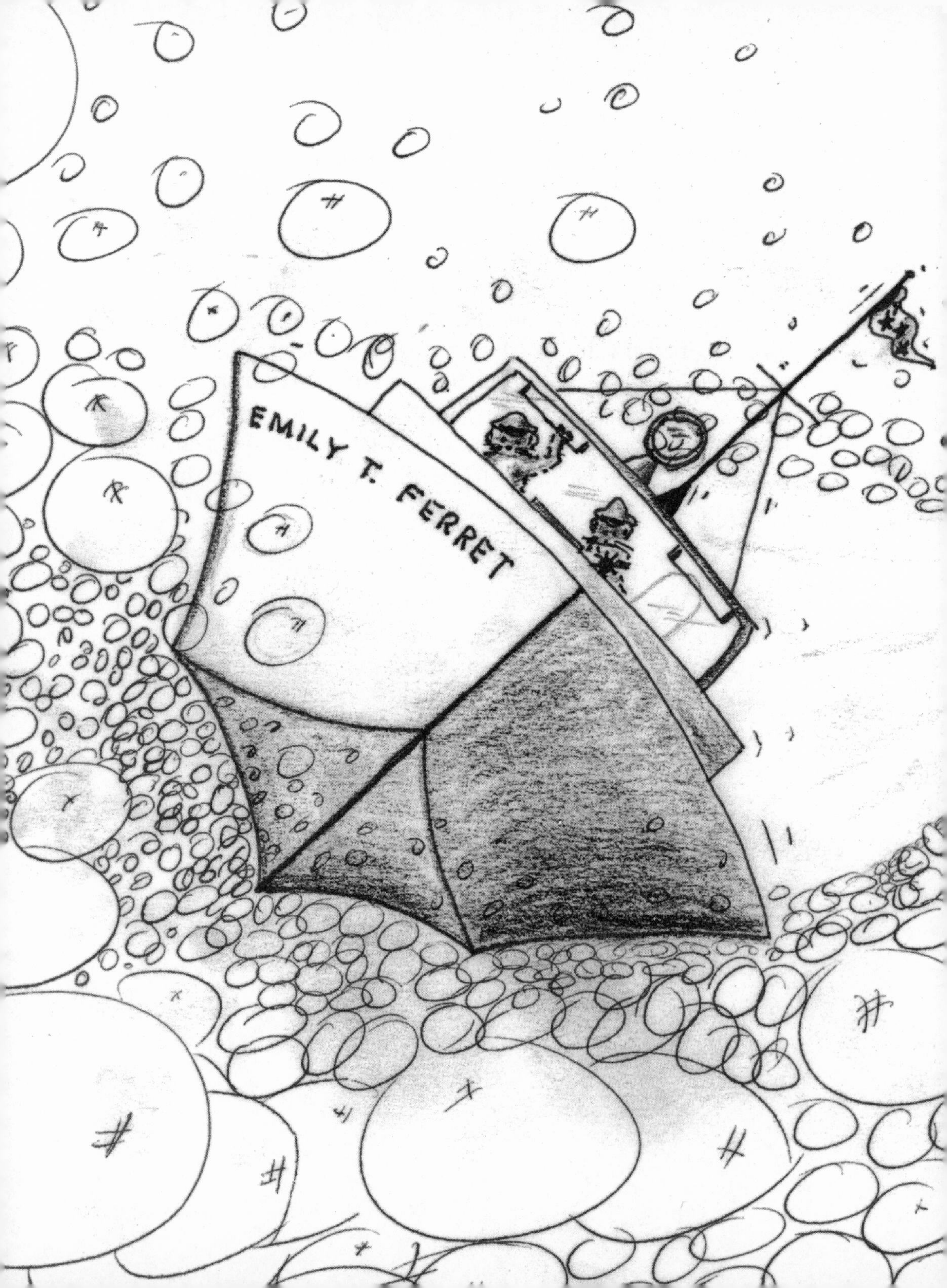
EMILY T. FERRET

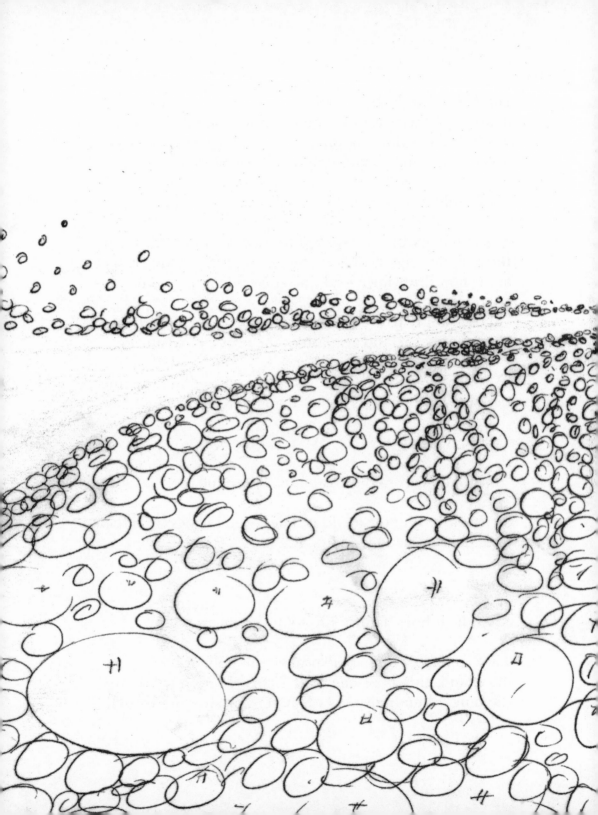

For a moment the black cliff of the freighter's hull loomed amid the snowy mass of foam, solid steel unmoving in the water but streaking midnight blurs alongside the high-speed ferret boat. Then it disappeared behind.

"Left rudder to course."

At last the rescue boat snaked its way, dead slow, through the reefs and shoals of Forbidden Island, Abington Ferret at the bow throwing a lead line and calling the depth.

"Mark, twenty paws!" he called. Then a toss and whistle of line in the air, and a splash as the boat moved ahead.

"Mark, fifteen paws!" Bubbles still blanketed the sea and the island, three times higher than the radar mast.

"Mark, twelve paws!"

"Anchor down," said the captain. "Siren, please."

Sharp blasts rent the air, four times over. Echoes from the invisible land nearby, and quiet.

"Again."

After the echoes, faintly, the sound of cheers.

The captain took the loudspeaker microphone. "Party on the island, this is rescue boat *Emily T. Ferret*. We are standing a hundred paws offshore, our siren every half minute. Approach to the edge of the water and our crew will pick you up. Do not swim for the boat. Our crew will pick you up."

The cheers came louder from shore, and "Hi! Hi!" from the survivors.

A few more siren blasts and Bosun's Mate Jingles Ferret appeared with the first of the wayward kits, bedraggled, covered in bubbles.

"Up you go, young fella," he said, lifting the kit to Joanna Ferret, the forward lookout, on deck. Then he turned back toward shore to retrieve the next of the adventurers.

The trip home to the rescue station took longer than the trip out. Though the bubbles had diminished, it was by no means a fit sea for more than half-cruise speed, even for a Ferret Rescue bubblebreaker.

As her mother turned the final page, the one with the picture of little Angela Ferret kissing Captain Terry, Bethany brushed back a tear, filled once more with admiration for the brave ferrets of the Rescue Service.

Her mother closed the book, and the room was silent. Then she rose and tucked their blankets close. "Good night, little ones."

Bethany took a breath, paused, spoke at last. "Someday, Mother, can I be a rescue ferret?"

Katrinka turned and beheld her daughter. Oh, my first-born, she thought. So like your father.

"You can be anything you want to be, my Betha-Nikka," she said, "if only you love enough." She kissed her two kits, turned out the light.

Far from the small stone house, in the highlands near the roof of the world, philosopher ferrets had learned the same and called it wisdom: we find our happiness only when we follow what we most love in all the world.

It was not the last time Bethany Ferret would hear her favorite story, but it was the first, listening to her mother, that she knew she would one day stand upon the deck of her own rescue boat.

CHAPTER 2

Not many humans know. On the edges of every sea, the Ferret Rescue Service stands with the Coast Guard and Coastal Patrol of every country that claims an ocean shore. It is the job of humans to rescue humans at risk in storm and shipboard disaster; it is the job of the ferrets to rescue seagoing animals in distress.

Adjoining each Coastal Patrol station lies a small base, home to those devoted and courageous ferrets who risk their lives to save others at sea. Ferret Rescue Service bases mirror the humans'—miniature living and dining quarters, maintenance bays and dry docks, and a small command center.

The FRS motto, *In Silentio Servamus,* tells its story. Quietly We Save: the goal and code of every animal who volunteers for the Service. They share a pride, these ferrets, that regardless of storm or oil or fire, rarely has a survivor of a stricken ship been lost once an FRS vessel has pulled alongside.

Their J-class rescue boats are small and light but strong, with powerful twin engines and fast on the water. Operated by a captain and crew of four sea ferrets, FRS rescue vessels have proven to be nearly unsinkable. In the course of their service, a few have been dragged down with shipwrecks or dashed to pieces in mountainous surf, but handled with skill and courage they are perfect for their mission.

Not so long after her mother had read her to sleep, having graduated from the arduous course of sea-ferret officer training, Ensign Bethany N. Ferret, FRS, reported for duty at the Maytime Rescue Base.

Maytime had been her choice by virtue of her standing at the top of her class. The base stood on a protected inlet along an otherwise rockbound coast, lashed in winter by ocean storms, surrounded in summer by a labyrinth of deadly currents. She had asked for action in service; at Maytime she was bound to get it.

She saluted. "Ensign Bethany Ferret reporting for duty, sir."

Commander Curtis Ferret looked up from the engine compartment of a J-boat, saw the trim figure dockside, returned her salute. First in her class, he thought, she's planning to be in command of her own boat before long. She's learned a lot, but there's so much more ahead. Poor kit. Lucky kit.

"What's the redline oil temperature for the engine of this boat, Ensign?"

Bethany was startled. She was expecting a welcome to the base, not a quiz.

"One hundred eighteen degrees Celsius, sir."

"What if the captain chooses to run the engine over-temperature?"

"Why, she can plan on the main bearings to seize, sir, she can plan on complete engine failure!"

The commander frowned, to cover his unseen smile. His new officer would command or die trying. "What if there are lives at stake, Ensign? What if she has to run her engines overtemp?"

"If she has to burn one, she'd best save the other, sir."

The senior officer surveyed the scorched metal. "That's what this captain did. Now we've got to rebuild the engine. And engines do not grow on bushes, Ensign."

"The captain saved how many lives, sir?"

He looked up sharply. "Twenty-five mice, three ship's cats, a pygmy marmoset. Twenty-nine lives."

"Yes, sir." His new officer stood at attention.

"Welcome to the base, Ensign," the commander said. "You picked some fine weather to report aboard. Enjoy it while you can." He turned back to the engine compartment. With the barometer falling, this boat would soon be called to service.

So began the adventure Bethany Ferret had sought. She was assigned as third officer aboard J-166, the rescue boat *Dauntless,* under the command of Captain Angio E. Ferret. From her first hour on board, she found the sea a more demanding classroom than any school she had known.

Always in some pre-dawn hour came rescue practice, over and again, in the sudden screeching whoop of the dockside alert siren. Amid the blasts, ferrets tumbled from hammocks into storm hats and life vests, scrambled for their stations. Sleep vaporized in the thunder of heavy engines bursting to life, darkness shattered in the arc of instant floodlights.

"Away the bowlines!" came the cry from the bridge. "Away the stern lines! Away the spring lines, away all lines! *All ahead, flank!*"

Twin searchlights stabbing ahead, twin hurricanes from the engines, white water flying from midships, sweeping into rooster tails astern.

From her station as Starboard High lookout, her face hidden in helmet and visor, Bethany raced through her station check, reporting herself ready for sea.

This is it! she thought. *Here's the life I wanted!* On the interphone, she listened to her captain call the Rescue Center.

"Maytime Control, J-166 is launched mid-channel seaward, standing by for vector and distance."

As often as not, that would be the end of the alert. "Roger, 166, your mid-channel time was fifty-eight seconds. This terminates the exercise. Return to base and stand by."

Other times, though, *Dauntless* would streak ahead, past the channel jetties into a sea of moonless black. She followed vectors from shore and her own lookouts to find some tiny motorboat or sailing vessel floating lights-out in the dark. Aboard, a crew of off-duty sea ferrets hiding belowdecks, curling themselves as small as possible, hoping to be overlooked by their rescuers.

"Seven survivors aboard, sir," Bethany had once reported, lookout turned rescuer, exhausted from dragging the dead weight of the distress-vessel animals to the deck of the *Dauntless.*

Angio Ferret had narrowed his eyes. Something was wrong. "We have all the survivors? Are you sure? Are all the survivors on board?"

The rescue would not be complete nor clock stopped until every creature in the practice was accounted for. She felt the captain's suspicion.

"Stand by, sir," she said. She dashed to the deck, past the survivors, relaxed and chatting now, forward of the bridge.

"Searchlight!" she called as she ran, and flew paw over paw down the stark-lit towline to the vessel just rescued. Scrambling aboard, she looked again from bow to stern. Just when she was certain there was no life on board, a shape in the sail locker caught her eye.

"All right," she said. "Come on, out you go!" Sure enough, a very young ferret had smuggled itself tightly under the canvas, scarcely daring to breathe. Bethany threw the sails aside, but even then the kit did not move, its eyes tightly shut.

"Gotcha." She lifted the youngster by the scruff of its neck, held it firmly in her teeth.

"I'm going to be a rescue ferret," it said in a tiny voice.

Bethany smiled in spite of herself. "Someday . . . ," she muttered.

The kit hung immobilized while she reappeared on deck, dashing up the towline over the waves into the glare of light. At last, aboard *Dauntless,* she set the kit with the other survivors, raced up the ladder to the bridge.

"Eight rescued aboard, sir," she panted.

"Are you sure, Ensign?"

"Yes, sir!"

The captain lifted his microphone. "J-166 has eight survivors aboard. The distress vessel is in tow."

"Roger, 166," came the reply. "Understand eight survivors. Exercise is terminated. Thirty-one minutes, twenty-five seconds. Return to base."

"Roger the time," said the captain, noting it in his log. "Returning to base."

He nodded to Bethany, releasing her to her lookout station.

"Oh, 166," came the voice from the Center, "can you tell us who found survivor number eight?"

The captain turned to his junior officer, puzzled by the question. "That was Ensign Bethany Ferret, located the last survivor."

"The very small survivor?" asked the voice on the radio.

Bethany nodded.

"That is affirmative," said the captain.

"Well done, *Dauntless*," said the Center. "Well done."

Angio Ferret nodded, a hint of a smile. There may have been a wager, he thought. He would not have been surprised to learn that survivor number eight had a close relative at the command center.

Bethany had run more than a dozen night missions before her first daytime alert.

Beyond her surprise at the alert siren going off in sunlight, the test was easier, she thought. She sighted the target vessel eleven minutes from the jetties, and though the seas were not smooth, *Dauntless* streaked top speed to its rescue station, lowered its skiff of rescuers, Bethany among them. The J-boat didn't require lookouts after the target was found.

Hard work, she thought. But her inner kit didn't care how hard it was. She had built this life from dreams in her hammock, and now the dreams were true.

Aloft once more in her lookout station, the distress boat in tow, Bethany saw the jetties from seaward for the first time in daylight, and what she saw stiffened her.

She pressed her interphone button, direct to the bridge. *"Vessel on the rocks!"* she called. "On the starboard jetty, sir!"

Waiting for the reply, her blood ran cold. That was no ordinary vessel, it was a rescue boat, a *J-boat,* stranded on the boulders!

She braced for the tilt of *Dauntless* to starboard, and the rush of her engines to aid. Neither happened.

Had the captain not heard? "Starboard High lookout to bridge, *we have a vessel on the rocks, sir!"*

"Roger, Starboard High," the captain answered. "The vessel's in sight."

Still J-166 proceeded at tow speed, her course unchanged.

Presently Bethany felt a movement behind her. She turned and saluted. "Welcome to Starboard High, sir!"

The skipper of *Dauntless* could be as tough and unyielding as the rocks themselves, a powerful animal who had worked his way from sea ferret third class to captain by native brilliance and devotion to the Service. As ever with the strongest of creatures, he rarely displayed his power, choosing courtesy instead, and understanding.

"At ease, Ensign." Angio Ferret touched her shoulder. "It's been there for a year now, Bethany," he said. "I thought I might tell you without your shipmates listening."

The lookout took her eyes from the gray wreckage, turned to him. "What happened, sir?" she asked. "Why?"

The officer sighed, lifted his cap and ran a paw through his fur. "She was returning from a night rescue, the seas were rough. More than rough . . . the channel radar buoy was dragged off station."

"But sir, she must have had the jetty on radar. . . ."

"By the time the captain realized what had happened, it was too late."

The younger ferret swallowed. "The crew, sir?"

"No one was lost. Survivors and crew jumped to the jetty and we picked them up straightaway. We left the wreck to remind us: Assume nothing. No mission's finished until our lines are fast to the dock."

Bethany watched the wreck, barely a hundred paws distant as *Dauntless* slid by. The bow showed above water at high tide, the name fading but legible: *Resolute.*

"But sir, the boat . . ."

"J-101 was the first of her class, the oldest vessel on station. We salvaged what we could. She's a good warning as we come and go. We won't lose another that way."

"But sir, the boat . . . ," she whispered.

The captain was down the ladder and returned to the bridge, yet Bethany's eyes stayed on the shattered metal stranded on the rocks. There was a yawning gash at the starboard waterline, a slice nearly half the length of the boat. The seas had jammed the hulk fast into the jetty. Most of *Resolute* went underwater on the high tides; she was pressed hard to the rocks on the lows. A lovely shape, sleek and trim despite the beatings, her twin lookout towers unscratched, defiant of the sea.

What a waste, the ferret thought. The oldest boat on the station, but so what? She's a *J-boat!* She can save lives!

⌢

Through her first tour, Bethany Ferret applied herself diligently to her duties as a sea-ferret officer. Night practice and day, emergency rescues, vessels in distress adrift at sea. The real events, though, were most of them less trying than the practice: vessels helpless, out of fuel at sea, vessels lost in fog, broken rudders and fouled propellers, animals to be rushed ashore.

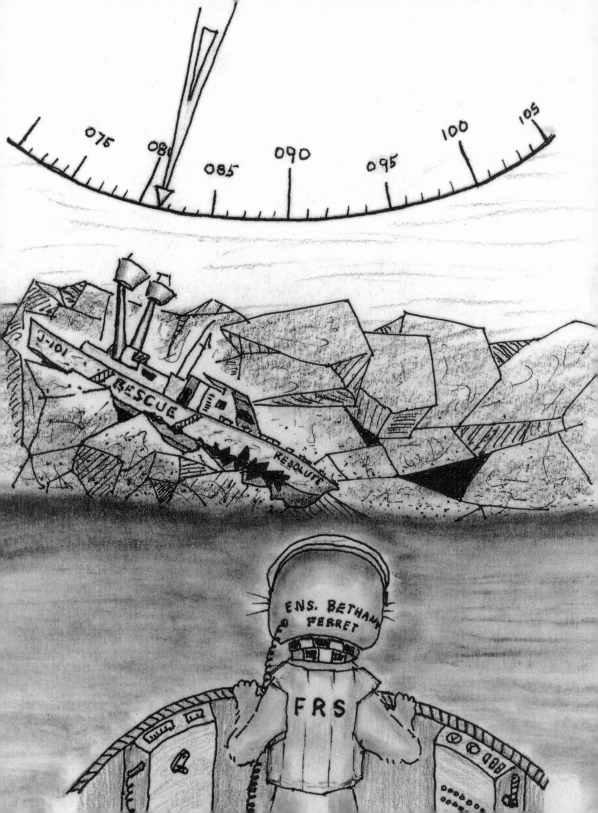

Now and then a major gale blew in, but most shipping stood warned in advance, steering to the safety of deep water, far from lee shores and jagged rocks of the storm-coast.

In time, Ensign Bethany Ferret was promoted to lieutenant junior grade, thence to full lieutenant. Her superior officers rated her skills and her attitude outstanding, her courage unwavering. Every one checked the square: "An exemplary ferret, one in a hundred, an officer I would wish to serve aboard my ship." Soon she was first officer aboard *Dauntless*.

Never did Bethany Ferret forget the sight of J-101 on the rocks. Every time she put to sea and every time she returned to base, the young lieutenant shook her head over the loss, stranded there.

It was not time, then, that moved J-101 from the teeth of the land, it was Bethany's patient, relentless pursuit of an ideal. The earnest young ferret never raised her voice over the issue, she never argued against other viewpoints.

No one taught her, but she knew: more important than talent or gifts or education is the determination to make one's wish come true. The young officer, quite simply, had resolved to rescue J-101, and she was willing to endure any hardship to see that happen.

"The value of *Resolute* to the Ferret Rescue Service is inestimable," she wrote, from her tiny quarters aboard

Dauntless. "Should this vessel be restored and save a single life, she would have paid for her own restoration. Should she save a hundred lives, there is no counting the return on the modest investment I propose."

In his office overlooking the docks, Commander Curtis Ferret turned the pages of her proposal, gray whiskers unmoving, his face impassive.

"I request that at little cost to the Ferret Rescue Service, on my own off-duty time and on the off-duty time of such sea ferrets who may wish to join me, that I receive permission to restore J-101, FRB *Resolute,* to alert-ready condition."

The base commander frowned. *Her captain has told her the wreck has a purpose,* he thought; *is this becoming an obsession? How can she save lives while she's rebuilding boats? She's a promising officer and her job is at sea.* Almost imperceptibly, he shook his head.

"At worst," Bethany wrote in her next letter, "the project will sharpen the knowledge and skills of its volunteers and make them better officers and sea ferrets. At best, the Maytime station will have an additional seaworthy, active-duty vessel to fulfill its mission requirements. This endeavor is in the best interests of the FRS, to save and protect seagoing vessels and animal lives aboard them."

The commander shook his head again, turned to gaze down from his office window at the boats that were his responsibility. He put her request aside.

Letter followed letter, as though *Resolute* were no derelict reminder but some enchanted sword-in-the-stone for an officer determined to pull her free for quests to come. Bethany Ferret made it clear that her wish was attainable, was valuable for the Rescue Service, that every aspect of her plan would be positive. Patiently she explained how she would overcome each test the project would offer.

On August 14, as her captain watched, Bethany took command of *Dauntless* on the rescue of two paddlers, hamsters drifted to sea by offshore currents, squeaking with joy at the sight of the ferret vessel pulling alongside. The seas were moderate; skill was required to take the paddlers and their craft aboard without harm or damage. *The lieutenant accomplished the rescue without incident,* Angio wrote in the ship's log, no other comment being necessary.

Upon her return to dock, a messenger found her aboard, saluted, presented her with a sealed envelope. Lieutenant Bethany Ferret was requested and required to appear at 1500 hours in the office of the base commander.

At 1459 hours she arrived, combed and brushed, trembling a little, a thick envelope of project plans under her arm.

She entered the commander's office precisely on time, saluted. "Lieutenant Bethany Ferret reporting as ordered, sir."

The commander nodded. "Sit down, Lieutenant." He turned in his chair, watched the docks, the row of sleek, snow-colored J-boats nosed into their berths, *Strongpaw* and *Courageous* on alert, closest to the sea, crews aboard, ready for immediate launch.

The office of the base commander, like the animal himself, was lean and polished. There were books in shelves on three walls, a fading photo of an old E-boat, Lieutenant Curtis Ferret standing proudly with his crew at the ladder to the bridge. On a cabinet, encased in glass, stood a scale model of a J-boat, finished to the smallest detail. Next to it a color picture of three kits tumbling on the grass at lakeside.

For a long while, the senior ferret did not speak. He turned back to his desk, glanced again at Bethany's service file, reviewed a line from her personal history: *Officer's father, Artemis Ferret, plunged from bridge into white-water rapids attempting solo rescue of two kittens adrift on river ice. Both animals in distress were pushed to paws of shore personnel, surviving without injury. Rescuer lost in freezing water.*

The commander stood, lifted a book that was open on his desk. "I have something to read to you, Lieutenant, from the FRS operations manual. Are you ready to hear this?"

Bethany sat erect on the edge of the wooden chair, her eyes watching his. "Yes, sir, I am."

"Then listen carefully, please." He turned a page. "'*Service policy forbids the personal involvement of officers in the construction, maintenance or operation of FRS vessels except in performance of duties to which they have been assigned by the Service.'"*

The senior ferret sighed and closed the book. "Do you have any comment?"

"Yes, sir." *Except in performance of duties assigned* could only mean one thing.

The commander nodded. "Go ahead."

"Thank you, sir!"

"So this is no surprise."

"No, sir. You had no choice, sir. Sooner or later you had to let me do it."

The commander shook his head, a smile of surrender. He lifted a sealed envelope from his desk, handed it forth.

"Your orders, Lieutenant, are to salvage, overhaul and return to service our vessel J-101, the Ferret Rescue boat *Resolute.* When the work is complete, you are to command that vessel for her sea trials and active-duty service. May I quote, to the best of my recollection?"

The young ferret grasped the envelope, tears in her eyes. "Of course, sir."

The commander turned again to the window, watched a returning J-boat drift slowly into its berth, ferrets on deck heaving its bow and stern lines ashore. *"As this endeavor is in the best interests of the FRS and its mission to save and protect seagoing vessels and animal lives aboard them, you are requested and required to complete your mission as soon as ingenuity and perseverance can provide."*

"Aye, aye, sir! Thank you, sir!"

She rose and stood wordless before him, wreathed in happiness. The commander gave her a salute of dismissal, to which she responded. Then she embraced the elder ferret in delight.

"Excuse me, sir," she said, recovering her dignity. "Thank you, sir. You'll be proud, sir. . . ."

"I'm already proud, Lieutenant. I'm expecting *Resolute* to stand alert this winter."

The young ferret caught her breath. It was an impossible schedule, to rebuild the boat and train a crew for rescue duty in two months' time.

"Aye, aye, sir!" She saluted and stepped toward the door.

"Oh, and one other thing."

Bethany turned. "Yes, sir?"

"If you need me to growl at somebody to make this happen, I trust you'll let me know."

She flashed a radiant smile. "I will, sir!"

Not the next week, as the commander had expected, but that very afternoon, magic began. Maytime's floating crane was somehow borrowed, and the hulk of *Resolute* was raised on slings from the rocks, by a crew of Bethany-charmed ferrets. By sunset the boat was in dry dock, red-tagged for express overhaul.

Not the next day but that evening the wreck swarmed with workers recruited by the lieutenant, unable to resist the intensity in those dark eyes when she came to them for help.

Welder ferrets' torches cut and patched, sparks and puddles of molten steel spilling firefalls through the night. A crew of burly sea ferrets heaving a hydraulic ram straightened and set crushed bulkheads; electricians tore looms of wiring from the sea-shattered bridge and replaced them with new. Armor-glass windows, overhauled instruments and electronics appeared at dockside as if by special delivery and were soon taken aboard. It was a steel orchestra swept over the edge of chaos: rivet guns, pneumatic hammers, high-speed grinding wheels, carpenter's saws, the boat crowded with every manner of specialist.

By dawn *Resolute*'s engines and generators had been winched free of the boat and trundled off to Powerplant Overhaul, her transmissions and driveshafts and propellers lifted out for inspection and balancing.

Shifts came and went as Bethany Ferret worked through, not noticing that she had tired at all. It was as though she had stored her sleep for this event; resolute as the boat she would command, she was everywhere at once, suggesting, ordering, flattering, pleading.

"You're saving lives," she told the engine ferrets below-decks. She hugged their chief, nearly twice her size. "Don't you want to be ready when the engines come back this afternoon, Boa? It's easier to check the radiators now than later. . . ."

"This afternoon, Lieutenant?" The big ferret smiled at her. "We only pulled 'em last week! They'll not be ready for ninety days!"

Bethany stood on tiptoe to whisper in his ear. "I traded our engines for two just out of overhaul."

The chief's eyes widened. His paw still on her shoulder, he called to his foreferret, "A move on, there, Billy! You want to get a good look at those cooling and exhaust systems right now, the fuel supply system, engine mounts and shaft bearings! Our lieutenant here tells me we got *lives* waiting on us!"

Noise engulfed the once-abandoned vessel, tools and fires and heavy-equipment engines, orders and commands flying, radios blaring the songs of WhitePaw, Dook and Zsa-Zsa and the Show Ferrets while all paws worked.

Gradually the haze around the dry dock changed from welding smoke to the flying dust of dry barnacles and old paint, then at last to a mist of new enamel, white as sea-spray, *Resolute* in black at her bows, *J-101* at her transom, *RESCUE* in flame-colored letters amidships.

At last, weeks from the afternoon she was taken from the rocks, the J-boat slipped back into the sea again, Lieutenant Bethany Ferret on the bridge. Her tail dragged with fatigue; she was thinner than she had been in the commander's office. Yet she trembled with excitement as her boat drifted loose-lined from dock. The ship's pennant fluttered in bright diagonal stripes, cherry-lemon colors flying from the crosstrees above, matching colors to the fresh crew-scarf tied neatly at Bethany's neck.

She pressed her interphone button. "Start Engine One, please, Boa."

"Starting One, ma'am," came the big ferret's voice in her headset.

The whir of the starter-motor, low at first, sliding swiftly up the scale to a sudden choking shudder, the whine blown away in heavy diesel thunder, rough and uneven for a moment, then quieter, smoother, the throttle drawn back.

She smiled. Life for my boat, she thought.

"Start Engine Two."

"Starting Two, ma'am."

The whir barely heard over the idle of the first engine, all at once J-101's second engine was firing, a faint cloud of black smoke from the exhaust. Bethany Ferret moved the telegraph handle forward.

"All engines ahead one-quarter."

"Ahead one-quarter, aye."

The boat trembled faintly, propellers turning.

She switched from interphone to the deck loudspeaker. "Away all lines," the officer said, her voice calm and even.

Mooring lines splashed into the water, hauled smartly aboard by paws from a volunteer crew.

A cheer went up from the pier, pride and relief, those exhausted animals glad with their new overhaul record, hoping not to see Lieutenant Bethany Ferret until they'd had a long rest.

Resolute's first trip was no more than a dozen boat-lengths, from dry dock to her berth alongside the other J-boats. There was much to be done before she'd be ready for sea: finishing crew and survivors' quarters belowdecks, crew selection and training exercises, sea trials for the boat and crew. A list of a hundred actions still needed before J-101 could back away from the berth into which she eased.

"All engines back a quarter," she said, spinning the helm hard to starboard.

"Back a quarter, aye."

Resolute inched sideways toward the rubber-shielded berth. "All engines stop."

"Engines stopped."

Now the boat drifted in silence. "Lines ashore," she said.

Ferrets sprang from deck to the land, fastened bow and stern and spring lines.

From the bridge to her hammock was only a few steps, yet Bethany barely made the distance. Her hat askew over her eyes, the gay new stripes of her crew-scarf still about her neck, she collapsed onto the blanket and fell instantly, profoundly asleep.

The fever of work continued in the days ahead, but at least, she thought, it's a fever I control. Instead of cajoling, pleading for the needs of her boat, Bethany was flooded in choices. She required four crew members. At once she had formal requests from a dozen sea ferrets and informal offers from a dozen more. An offer even from Boa, the big chief engine ferret from dry dock, who once had sworn he wanted a hammock on land and never go back to sea.

Her volunteers had watched her breathe her spirit into J-101, had seen her drag the vessel back to life by her own fierce will. They knew that she would demand as much of them: three paws for the boat and one paw for yourself, still they applied to serve under the young officer, so much did they admire her spirit.

In her cabin, Bethany had studied their résumés over and again, interviewed, watched the eyes and hearts of those who would be her crew.

The last application was from Ensign Vincent Ferret, arrived yesterday from Sea Ferret Officers' School, following his sister to Maytime.

She set it down and sighed. Oh, Vink, she thought. If I take you aboard, someday I'll be ordering you into danger, maybe into death. I'll never do that.

His application rejected, herself nearly asleep, she heard his voice in her mind: "I chose this life same as you did, sis. If I'm not under your command I'll be under somebody else's, same risks. I'll trust you more, work harder for you than for anyone. I'll do whatever you ask. Let me come!"

She shook her head and slept. In her dreams she watched herself slip *Resolute*'s candy-stripe crew-scarf about her brother's neck, and still asleep, she murmured, frightened for what she had done.

CHAPTER 3

Not days were the pages of Bethany's diaries, nor months. She measured her life by events: by storms at sea, by vessels in distress. Not December 20, but the sinking of the *Mary Louise Ferret* and the rescue of no less than 328 crew, passengers and stowaway mice. Next, the shepherding of the *Queen Angela* into port when her rudder failed. Next, the saving of every ship's animal from the humans' deep-sea trawler *Lydia Shepard* before she capsized and went to the bottom.

When the alert siren sounded under gale flags, crews human and ferret fired their engines and launched between the Maytime jetties into the tempest, racing each other to be first to the vessel in distress. Ferret rescue boats were smaller but lighter, with greater power for their weight. In smooth seas they outran the humans' Coast Guard cutters, but in high seas and gale winds, great skill was required for the J-boats to win the race.

On station, the boats worked together, helping crippled vessels to port, standing by to save lives when ships went down. This job, for Bethany, made her life worth living.

Then, storm season nearly over, a strange order from the base commander. Bethany opened the envelope, read the single page and frowned. The crew of *Resolute* was requested and required to host one Chloe Ferret, a journalist on assignment to tell the stories of ferrets at risk. The commander trusted that Lieutenant Bethany N. Ferret would show all due courtesy to the visitor, as she would be responsible for the journalist's safety and comfort during her stay.

Bethany's heart fell. In the privacy of her quarters aboard ship, she dropped the orders on her tiny desk, leaned against her hammock. It's hard enough, she thought. Hard enough with survivors in panic, abandoning ship before they need to, hard enough with the seas, with waves higher than my boat. Now I need to do it with a *writer* on board?

She would have appealed to the commander, but such was her gratitude to him for command of *Resolute* that she responded that it would be her pleasure to host the journalist.

Boa asked it first, the crew assembled on deck to hear the orders: "Is this *the* Chloe Ferret, Cap'n? The same Chloe Ferret from Zsa-Zsa and the Show Ferrets?"

"Of course not," said Bethany. "That one's a singer, isn't she?"

"She's *famous,* ma'am!" said Dhimine Ferret, *Resolute*'s Starboard High lookout and youngest of the crew. "Zsa-Zsa and the Show Ferrets are, well, celebrities! Chloe writes, too, for the big magazines."

"It's true, Captain," said Vincent Ferret. Her brother ever took care to address Bethany by her proper titles: *lieutenant* onshore, *captain* on board. Were the crew not so small, they would never have guessed the two were related. "She wrote a story about space ferrets in orbit, not long ago. She seems to like danger. Or maybe the appearance of danger, ma'am. I shouldn't say that rescue is exactly dangerous."

"She can sing for me," said Harley Ferret. "She can sing for me whenever she wants." Harley was *Resolute*'s Port High lookout and the most reckless animal of the crew. Sleek and dashing along the very edge of sea-ferret regulations, occasionally flying over the bounds, Bethany had chosen him for his sheer daring, his choices to risk his life time and again to rescue animals at sea. More than once she had shielded him from consequences that would have grounded any other ferret—it was thanks to her that he still wore his crew-scarf.

"Fine with me," said Boa. "So long as she stays in her place, doesn't get in the way."

Bethany nodded. "When she wants to talk with us, we talk. I want you to tell it as it is, I want you to answer her questions. Just a few wild stories, Harley, not too many. If she wants to go along on training, she can. She'll stay with me on the bridge. When we get a rescue call, though, she goes ashore. After we're home we'll tell her the story, what happened, how we felt about it, whatever she wants to know."

Bethany Ferret did not often underestimate others. The truth, however, was that her young lookout was right— Chloe Ferret was a star. Wrapped in the world of her boat and her mission, Bethany did not imagine what that was to mean on the high seas.

CHAPTER 4

T HE KNOCK on Bethany's cabin door was neither soft nor demanding.

"I'm looking for my room. . . ." The ferret who stood before her was dark and beautiful, her fur carefully brushed, whiskers combed. Her eyes were bright and inquisitive under a navy-style designer hat that would have set the lieutenant back a month's salary. "They told me this would be my ship."

"You must be Chloe," Bethany replied, offering her paw to the lovely creature, charmed in spite of herself. "I'm the captain. Welcome aboard."

"You're very young to be a captain, aren't you?"

The rescue ferret sighed. "Young but determined, they tell me."

The singer looked at her carefully, reading Bethany's eyes in the silence. Then she smiled, a warm hello. "We're going to be friends, aren't we?"

Bethany nodded, smiled back. "As long as you do everything I ask."

"I promise, Captain. Could you show me my room?"

"Of course. It's not far away, onshore. You'll have the VIP suite in the visiting officers' quarters. To be pre- ferred, Miss Chloe, over sleeping on the boat."

"Call me Clo, please," the show ferret replied. "When I'm on a story, though, I don't sleep in suites. I need the experience, the real thing. I'd rather not be an observer."

"This time, you might want the suite. Crew's quarters are assigned, of course. Survivors' quarters are not what we call luxurious. In fact, they're a little bare."

"They'll be fine. I'll just drop my bag and then could I meet your crew?"

Bethany shrugged, led the other down the companionway forward nearly to the chain locker, opened a door on the right, touched a light switch. "There's not much view, I'm afraid."

"Thank you. I didn't come for the view. I came to live your life."

The officer smiled at the audacity. "Happy to share it. Most of it, anyway: the routine, the training. Of course you won't join us when we're called on rescue, you understand."

"The regulations forbid it," said Chloe, "you can't be responsible for an observer in the way, you need as much room for survivors as possible."

"Exactly. The storm season's nearly over. But you'll find our training realistic."

There were no questions, the two understood each other perfectly. Storm season or not, Chloe Ferret had come to report a rescue firsthand, every exciting second of it, and she fully expected to do that. Bethany, for her part, was quite prepared to lock the writer onshore to keep her from endangering lives at sea.

Yet the young officer knew that the rock star's story would be in the best interests of the Service, that it would be read by thousands of kits ready to decide their lives and perhaps by a few ready to risk them for others.

The two emerged from the forward companionway at the moment that Boa came up the aft ladder from the engine room. In the instant that the engine ferret raised his paw to salute the officer, his eyes caught the visitor's, and he extended the salute, politely, to include her. He didn't notice that for a second, as their eyes met, she had stopped breathing.

Chloe turned her head to watch the big animal as he passed. "And he would be . . . ?"

"That's Boa," said Bethany. "Without Boa, you and I wouldn't be standing on this deck."

The reporter turned to look again, but the ferret was gone. Normally, she would have held her tongue, but she had liked the officer at once, and she spoke her heart: "Bethany," she asked, "do you love him?"

The lieutenant laughed in surprise. The kind of question that makes good stories, she thought. "I love all my crew, Chloe. Of course I love Boa."

"The oddest thing, Captain," said the rock star, puzzled, shaking her head. "So do I."

Through the afternoon, Bethany found that it was easy to be nice to her guest. A strange animal, she thought, testing her intuition. On one paw vivacious, engaging, open, charismatic. On the other she's shy, even a little frightened.

That evening, at the door to the station mess hall:

"After you," said Bethany. "Our crew table is on the port side . . . that's on the left."

But instead of entering, her beautiful visitor waited, shivered. "Give me a minute."

The lieutenant turned and stared. "Are you all right?"

"Fine," she said. "I need a second to breathe, to get ready." Then a quick smile of apology. "No matter how much you love other animals, you build walls when too many get too close. I need to tell myself to let down the walls."

Then Chloe squared her shoulders, took a breath and entered the Maytime Rescue Station mess hall, as poised as for the cover of *Rolling Stoat*.

At once conversation stopped, echoes dying away. Nearly a hundred faces turned to the door, every eye stared, unbelieving, absolute silence.

Chloe Ferret? *The* Chloe Ferret? *In the Maytime mess hall?*

The situation balanced on its edge. In a second there could have been a stampede of fans.

"Carry on," said Bethany, her voice firm and clear in the silent confusion. "Miss Chloe appreciates your welcome." She led the way, striding to the table by a towering steel placard, polished as a knight's shield, ebony letters under a field of stripes in red and yellow: *J-101 Resolute.*

With that, after a startled quiet, conversation returned to the room, though Bethany suspected the buzz of voices was about who had just walked through the door. A little fame must be sweet, she thought, but too much, I'll bet too much is a cake, stuffed down your throat.

Ensign Vincent Ferret, who had been chatting with his shipmates, sat up smartly when his sister arrived. "Crew table, 'tench-*hut!*"

The four animals stiffened in place, braced upright, eyes straight ahead, unmoving, around a table fairly loaded with food.

"At ease, *Resolute*," said Bethany, and her crew relaxed, turned to listen. She took her place at the head of the table, touched the empty chair to her right for their guest.

"You know Chloe Ferret," she said. "She doesn't know you."

From the other side of the table, her brother rose and nodded. "First Officer Vincent Ferret, ma'am. Glad to have you with us."

The chief engine ferret, twice the bulk of the first officer, struggled, half-rising. "We've met. Call me Boa, ma'am."

"I'm Harley," said the raffish sea ferret. He looked directly into her eyes, an instant longer than was quite proper.

"Dhimine," said the smallest ferret breathlessly, glancing away.

"The finest crew in the Rescue Service," said Bethany, firm and proud.

"Then I've come to the right place," said Chloe. "I want to know what it means to be the finest. I want to know what it's like to be you."

There was an awkward silence. Boa broke it without a word. He lifted a platter of zucchini-lemon fettuccine in one paw, a bowl of Sicilian summer salad in the other, offered them to their guest with a hint of a smile.

"We eat well," he said.

Their visitor laughed.

"What's it like to be us?" said Dhimine shyly. "Practice, practice, practice."

Harley nodded, helped himself to golden spaghetti pie and Mediterranean wheat-berry rolls. "You'll see. On a nice day, nothing we do is hard. The hard part's doing it at night, searchlights only go a hundred paws in the rain, less in the snow, the wind blowin' force nine, the tops of the waves in your teeth . . ."

"Some snow peas, Harley?" Bethany smiled, offered the cool distraction to her lookout.

He touched his chest, inclined his head politely in gallant response, accepted the tender greenery.

Chloe's eyes widened. "It's that bad?"

"No," said Boa, snapping a carrot stick in one huge paw. He grinned at the handsome lookout. "It's only that bad when there's a lady to impress."

"Tell her, Harley," said Bethany. "It's mostly routine, isn't it?"

The lookout nodded, chastened. "Yes, ma'am." He turned to Chloe, caught by those beautiful eyes. "Mostly we're an escort for a boat that's low on fuel, or one that's a little lost, or somebody's not feeling well, they need to get to shore in a hurry. Not a very exciting life. Routine, like the skipper says, mostly." His glance fell to his plate.

"Mostly routine," said the rock star, "but not always?" Her smile would have melted any animal.

Harley looked up happily, shrugged. "Not always."

"The rest is practice, Miss Chloe," said Dhimine. "Engine start and castoff, against the clock. First boat to clear the jetty. First boat to the rescue site. Lost Mouse, how many minutes to find him."

"It's always against time, Clo," Bethany explained, pouring high-mountain ice water for their guest. "Don't worry if you left your stopwatch at home, there are plenty on board."

The visitor lifted her head and looked about the room, seeing mostly eyes watching her. The tall shields distinguished the tables of the rescue crews, each animal wearing the bright silk scarves of her or his own boat's colors.

Under a field of yellow and blue lightning bolts: *J-131 Defiant.*

Red and green triangles: *J-139 Heavensent.*

Green and yellow polka dots: *J-143 Courageous.*

White and black diamonds: *J-160 Strongpaw.*

Blue and white checkerboard: *J-166 Dauntless.*

Gold and black stripes: *J-172 Stormhaven.*

How must it feel, Chloe wondered, to see those names appear from the gloom, in freezing wild black water, when one is near dying terrified? Could my story open there, out in the dark?

"Every crew's the best," she whispered.

Boa nodded. "To the poor soaked creatures they haul out of the sea, Miss Chloe, you bet they're the best!"

CHAPTER 5

CHLOE APOLOGIZED for the hour she spent signing autographs after dinner, her baked stuffed pear untouched, her fragrant panforte barely nibbled despite its wondrous colors and spices. Then she and *Resolute*'s crew walked together from the mess hall to their boat, the moon and dock lights glimmering on the water alongside. It was low tide, the air thick with the smell of salt and the sea.

Dhimine asked shyly if Chloe planned to write a song about *Resolute*.

"Not a song," she said. "A story. I've always wondered about you. A lot of ferrets wonder who you are, what it's like. I want to tell the story."

"I wonder about *you,*" said Dhimine. "I wonder about Zsa-Zsa and Mistinguette. Are you really like what they say in *Celebrity Ferrets?*"

Chloe laughed. "The press doesn't always print the whole story. Everybody thinks she's this wild ferret, but Zee-Zee's no party animal, not a bit. She reads. Ferret history. Archaeology. She loves old things. 'History is us-then calling to us-now,' she says."

Harley choked. "You're kidding! Zsa-Zsa the Show Ferret? She *reads?*"

"Encyclopedia with paws," said Chloe into the shocked silence. "And Mistinguette . . . Misty's got a heart as big as all outdoors. Our romantic. She's writing lyrics, singing, dancing, but all the time she's waiting for Mr. Wonderful to say hello and help her lift the world."

The gentlest of breezes whispered of summer coming.

"And what would they tell us," asked Bethany, "about you, Clo?"

The lovely brow furrowed for a moment. "'Clo's always moving,' they'd say. 'She's restless. She's looking for something she's never found.'"

The six animals boarded *Resolute,* each but one touching its cap with a paw, a salute to the **FRS** flag flying from the crosstrees over the bridge. Beyond lay the night, the stars glittering cool and careless above.

Good-nights, and the captain led the writer to her place in the survivors' quarters. "And what Clo's looking for is . . . ?"

Her guest paused at the door. "I don't know, Bethany." She touched the officer good-night, watched her as one friend watches another. "Do you know beauty that's beyond anything we can imagine? It's there, I know. One time, I want to see that beauty."

CHAPTER 6

OVER THE NEXT weeks Bethany found that Chloe Ferret was no write-and-run journalist. Days she spent with the crew, helping as they buffed and polished *Resolute,* watching and listening from out of the way as they checked the boat's systems over and again.

She stood behind the captain on the bridge for the daily pre-patrol inspections, listened to her on the interphone.

"Starboard High station check, please."

"Main searchlight, on . . . ," came Dhimine's voice over the speakers, and the light from her tower blazed, glaring even in daylight. ". . . and off. Secondary is on . . . and off. Smoke flares, parachute flares, dye-markers and line-launchers are loaded and safe, circuit lights are green. Life raft is stored and safe. Pelorus—three-six-zero degrees . . ."

Chloe watched the compass-bearing indicator marked *Starboard High* swing through its dial in quarter-circle jumps as the lookout tracked her instrument around the horizon.

"What's a pelorus?" she asked.

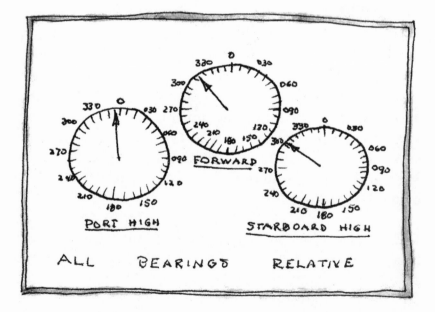

Bethany touched the indicator. "It points to landmarks."

". . . two-seven-zero, and three-six-zero. Autocamera power is on, covers are off. Starboard High is ready for launch."

The captain clicked her stopwatch, noted the time without comment. "Port High station check," she called.

"Main searchlight is on . . . ," came Harley's voice.

Bethany insisted that each of her crew be trained to fill the duties of the other, that any of them be able to command the boat, if necessary. She required that each crew member school the others on his or her own station, which meant mainly that she and Boa held classes in engine operation and seaferretship.

Resolute held her own practice sessions when she was not standing alert duty, Dhimine and Harley on the bridge, easing the boat from the dock and running it high cruise on autopilot and radar to practice rescues, Boa firing line-launchers until he could lay a rescue rope on a bell-ball floating barely visible in the water.

Chloe listened and watched, even steered the boat from time to time. She pointed searchlights in the dark, then turned them off, once, and fired a parachute flare high above, to see how it felt.

"Like setting loose a great slow comet over the water," she wrote. "With a touch of my paw I turned night into noon for two minutes fourteen seconds."

Before long, secretly, she began to believe that she could run the boat herself, if she had to. Still she studied. Alongside her hammock in the survivors' quarters were research books: *History of the Ferret Rescue Service, Strategy and Tactics of Small-Animal Rescue at Sea, The Sea Ferret's Manual, Marine Engine Operator's Handbook, Small Boats in Heavy Seas, Lessons in Twin-Screw Boat-Handling, Ferret Heroes: Amazing Stories from the FRS.*

"You're happy here, Boa," she had said on one visit to the engine room. "You know this place, you love it. How many animals live lifetimes without finding what they love?"

The big ferret had looked up at her along the oiled side of the injector block he was installing. "I couldn't say, Miss Chloe," he had replied, "but it's my job to find it for me."

How we learn from our choices, thought the journalist, and how determined we are to practice our lessons!

"My mother told me," Vincent said as they returned late from night-rescue practice, "and I never forgot." He paused for a long while, the two of them watching the luminous spray fly from amidships. "'Vink, if you want to meet the one ferret who can fix any trouble, no matter how bad it is, the one who can bring you happiness when nobody else can do it—why, just look in the mirror and say hello.'"

"You can learn a lot about an animal," Chloe wrote that night, "when you find what gives it comfort." Bethany's comfort, she thought, came from welding separate animals into a disciplined, powerful force of love, then pitting that force against the elements. That was the core of her skill as a sea-ferret officer. The captain needed to know that love could conquer all, and she was willing to bet her life, if need be, to prove it.

Though Chloe filled a second notebook, and a third, in time she came to feel more one of *Resolute*'s family than a visiting outsider. If she had to be an observer, she thought, she'd be an intimate one.

Chloe eased so smoothly into the crew that the captain barely noticed the change. Boa taught the journalist the art of knots, and she practiced incessantly, till she could tie a Monkey's Fist in seconds, throw clove hitches like magic tricks, whip a bowline on a line's end with the snap of her wrist.

Boa confided that he had spent a summer in Montana, when he was a kit, at Monty Ferret's Rainbow Sheep Resort and Ranchpaw Training Center. Not a secret, yet a fact that he had shared with no one but the captain before. He told sea stories to the rock star, and when his

Truth Fairy said the moral after each in a tiny mouse-voice (". . . and that's why we *never* leave open barrels of honey balanced on our engine hatches"), she laughed so that she leaned against him, helpless in tears.

One day, returning from practice at cruise speed, Bethany and Chloe stood alone on the bridge.

"Thank you, Captain."

"You're welcome, Clo." Bethany pressed her interphone button. "All ahead three-quarters, Chief, if you will."

"Ahead three-quarters, aye," replied Boa, the engines a wall of thunder behind his voice.

The rumble belowdecks rose and the boat lunged forward, its keel lifting. Glowing water flashed away to port and starboard, snow blasted across a sea the color of blurring ebony.

"Thanks for letting me in," said the writer. "I'm not used to that."

The captain grinned. "Everybody lets you in, Clo," she said. "They love you! You're magic!"

She touched the interphone selector. *"Lookouts for the jetty."*

"Port High," said Harley.

"Starboard High," said Dhimine.

Two pelorus repeaters swung to point a few degrees right of course. Followed by the third, from Ensign Vincent Ferret's position at the bow.

"Forward lookout's on the jetty," he called.

Bethany held *Resolute* on course, planning a right-angle entry to the channel. She could have navigated by radar, but electronics can fail, she knew, and when that happens only practice and skill can guide a boat.

"If celebrity's magic," said Chloe, "it's a screen, and I'm forever outside. Whatever I do that's not what they expect me to do, whatever I say that's not what they want me to say, they're disappointed; I'm not who they hoped. I wish sometimes somebody would see *me* and not some . . . some mirror flash they want me to be."

"I don't think you're a mirror flash," said Bethany. "I don't think Boa does. Or even Dhimine, anymore. She's over being shy, she tells you her secrets."

"That's why my thanks, Captain."

The officer touched the bill of her working cap, her rescue-cap, marked and creased now with sun and salt and practice. "We're here to serve."

As the days passed, Bethany forgot that Chloe Ferret was not a product of the sea-ferret training system, that her discipline was personal and not Service-taught. The captain forgot, in short, that Chloe was not her crew, she was a rock star.

CHAPTER 7

O N APRIL 17, the vessel *Deepsea Explorer* turned from the Gulf of Alaska, following the gray whale migration course west of Canada, measuring the currents along the way, comparing temperatures with the ocean surrounding, counting plankton. It was the last leg of a voyage filled with discovery.

Aboard were one calico cat, a Shetland sheepdog, an Indonesian parrot, seventy-six ship's rats and thirty-five mice who had crept aboard seeking adventure where they could find it.

Also aboard were forty-four humans, crew and scientists, each with a thousand questions for the oceans and the distant skies. Like electronic nets, computer disks once blank were now stuffed with answers. Secure in sealed containers lay fresh discoveries about animal life from the trees of Malaysia to the depths of the Mindanao trench, whispers from the planet's farthest atmospheres. Caught in those disks was the last cry from the sea to the creatures who depend upon it for their lives.

The low-pressure system that moved in from the west as they passed Vancouver Island and the Strait of Juan de Fuca was at first no more than a curl on the horizon, an apostrophe to a successful voyage. No one ashore or at sea expected that strange sky to be any more than a photo opportunity for satellites.

In four days, though, *Deepsea Explorer* wallowed not so far to windward of the rocks north of Maytime, pounded by force-eight winds and giant swells beyond the ship's capacity to resist. From time to time, the bow of the ship was lifted and balanced aloft in empty air, till *Explorer*'s seams began to part forward and her pumps could no longer keep the ocean out. Not long past midnight, she called for escort, for a rescue ship to stand alongside for safety.

Minutes later, her stern lifting clear in a sudden monster wave, came a thuddering screech of spinning, failing steel that deafened the storm itself. Bent while turning nearly full speed, the starboard propeller shaft tore itself apart, shearing great holes in the ship as it did, water flooding forward.

The call for escort changed. "Mayday, Mayday, Mayday! This is *Deepsea Explorer, Deepsea Explorer*. We have lost our starboard propeller shaft, we have lost our rudder, the forward hold and engine room are flooding. Our position is three-point-two miles on the two-six-two-degree bearing from the Moray Reef radio beacon. We have forty-four souls on board. Mayday, Mayday, Mayday. This is *Deepsea Explorer. . . ."*

At that moment the radio failed, its antenna shattered by flying debris. But the message was out, and at once the Maytime sirens wailed into the night.

One second asleep in her hammock, the next second Lieutenant Bethany Ferret tumbled to the deck, coming awake as she raced to *Resolute*'s bridge. Snapping the interphone on, she paused to calm her voice, then spoke as though this were just another practice.

To the engine room she called, "Boa, start Engine One, start Engine Two." She did not inquire whether the chief engine ferret was awake or ready with a quarter-minute warning from the sirens.

She switched to the ship's loudspeaker. "Topside crew, paws on deck. We have a vessel in distress, this is not a drill." Her words amplified, echoed below, and the crew burst down the companionway to their posts.

"Chloe Ferret, ashore at once, please; Chloe, get ashore now, please!"

With the first siren, the rock star woke in a haze of confusion; now the loudspeaker called her name. They can't be launching the boat! She dropped from her hammock, unbelieving. No ferret in her right mind would even *think* of . . .

Already engines shuddered to life beneath her.

"Stand by to cast off," said the loudspeaker. Then: "Cast off the bow line."

Chloe staggered up the companionway.

"Cast off the stern line."

The journalist stopped, clung to the pawrail. She was still asleep, too frightened to move. Storm season's past. Practice is nearly always in quiet water.

The loudspeaker continued, insistent. "Chloe Ferret, ashore at once, please." Then, sharply: *"Clo, get ashore!"*

She froze on the steps. This has to be a dream.

"All engines back one-quarter."

Resolute began to move, Chloe could feel it beneath her. In this storm, the boat was going to sea!

"Cast off the spring lines."

She listened to it all, her paws clenched, saw herself in the companionway as though she were an observer far away, watching her own life as it happened.

"Engines ahead one-quarter. Crew to stations, jackets and harness. Forward lookout, give me a searchlight, please. All engines ahead one-half . . . all engines ahead three-quarters."

Resolute began to pitch on the waves, gathering speed, though she had barely left dockside.

Chloe staggered back to the survivors' quarters, found her life jacket, slipped it on. Then she stopped, and began to tremble.

On the bridge, Bethany felt the keen edge of the storm, the edge of the wildest weather she had known, and she pressed into it nearly at top speed.

"Starboard High, Port High, give me main searchlights on the jetty forward. All lookouts, your station checks, please."

Practice, practice, practice, Dhimine had said. Now it was her voice on the interphone, calm and even to her captain. "Main searchlight, on. Secondary is on . . . and off. Smoke flares, parachute flares, dye-markers and line-launchers are loaded and safe, circuit lights are green . . ."

The captain listened to the checks, marked the position of the distress vessel on her chart, guessed her compass course to the site, set the autopilot to Heading Hold but did not engage it, preferring to steer *Resolute* by paw.

With the sound of pebbles on steel, rain fired against the topsides and armor glass. Under the searchlights, the downwind side of the channel was white water, breakers nearly burying the rocks as J-101 raced seaward.

This is going to be interesting, Bethany thought. Already she was planning her approach to the distress vessel, visualizing the positions ahead. If we hold station on the leeward side, forward if possible, she thought, that will leave room for the Coast Guard cutters to work the midships and aft sections, but it will put us between the ship and the shore, not much time for us to search for animals. If we hold station to windward, it'll give us more time to work, but the seas will be rougher. . . .

"Hello, *Resolute,* this is *Strongpaw.* We're in the channel outward bound. We do not have your lights in sight. Say your position."

Bethany spoke to the interphone, "High lookouts, give me your secondary lights aft, down the channel."

The two searchlights blazed over the wake as the boat flew between the jetties.

The captain lifted the interphone, spoke to Captain Chester Ferret, a Canadian animal on exchange duty at Maytime. "Hello, *Strongpaw*. *Resolute* is at Marker Four, we've got lights aft for you."

A long silence. "Nothing in sight, Bethany. What's your speed?"

"We're ahead full. Forty knots."

Another silence, longer still. "See you at the rescue site, hey?"

For a second, as *Resolute* cleared the end of the jetties, Bethany thought the boat had run aground. The sea was a cratered moonscape, sudden cliffs high above her radio mast, yawning caverns under her keel. Breakers sledged against the bow as though they would hammer it flat. She couldn't force her way through this sea at high speed.

"All engines ahead standard," she called to the engine room.

"Ahead standard, aye," Boa replied, easing the throttles back. At once the boat slowed, the pounding not so vicious as it had been.

"How are you doing, Forward?" she called.

"No problem, ma'am," said her brother, watching the dark at the tops of the seas through night-vision lenses. "Distress vessel is not in sight."

I love you, Vink, the captain thought.

"Hello, lookouts, we are three miles from the last reported position. Our time en route is twelve minutes, could be less if she's drifting downwind. We have no radar contact and we may not get it for a while. Look sharp."

CHAPTER 8

ABOARD *Deepsea Explorer,* the mice and ship's rats watched the known world slant downward. Jasper Rat, though not the eldest, had spent more time at sea than anyone, and the others turned to him, eyes wide. What did it mean, the terrible screeching noise, this vast tilting of the deck, salt water flooding where water had never been?

"We're going to be all right," he said. "We're close to shore, and if the ship is in danger we can hope for rescue. They'll take us under tow to port." He looked at the anxious faces about him, more than a hundred rodents, the mice already trembling. "If the water reaches B deck, we may lose the ship, and I want you all to get forward to the chain locker, up the anchor chain to the hawsehole, and hold on tight. I'll take Sammy with me, and we'll go there now ourselves. The rescue ferrets will need all the help we can give, to get us out of here."

"What if the ferrets don't come, Jasper?"

"The ferrets always come."

The mouse shuddered. "If they don't?"

"Then we jump from the hawsehole and we swim for it."

"Jasper, I can't swim!"

"Then you hold my paw and we jump together."

Another voice from the back. "I can't swim, either. . . ."

"When a ship is in trouble, the ferrets will come," said the sea rat firmly. "And when they hoist the rescue cage up to us, I don't want any me-first and I don't want any panic. I want the youngest animals on the first load down to the ferrets, and I expect the rest of you to stay calm. The mice, all other animals next, sea rats last. Nobody jumps from this ship unless I tell them to jump."

"Will they rescue the cat?"

"They'll rescue all of us. The cat won't hurt us when the ship is in danger. It's the law of the sea." He did not wait for further questions. "Sammy, let's go."

⌣

Belowdecks on *Resolute,* Chloe Ferret was wide-awake. Ferrets are not often seasick but they can be frightened. She knew it was worse for her, that every other animal on board had a job to do, they could cling to their duty. She could only cling to her hammock support and wait it out.

She had taken Harley's storm stories for fiction. How grateful she was now, in the midst of the storm, for Vincent's patient lessons about the strength of the J-boats, how few were lost at sea. Vincent had shown her with drawings and equations that it was nearly impossible for surface water to crush a hull of *Resolute*'s size and design. There was little danger so long as they kept clear of rocks and shoals and sinking ships. All she had to do, she thought, was hang on.

Chloe decided that she could at least watch the action from a better place, and stumbled down the tossing deck toward the companionway and up the ladder, gripping the pawrails. Before she opened the hatch to the deck, she grasped the safety hook of her harness tightly in one paw. There was a steel cable on the bulkhead aft of the entrance, she knew, and she'd snap the hook fast the instant she was out the hatch, just as Boa had taught her in practice.

As the boat rolled starboard, she pressed the handle and pushed hard on the door. At once she was thrown nearly overboard. Black water surged about her knees, her hat disappeared in a half second. But she was ready and she knew where the line waited. By the time the sea swept her off her paws, she was fastened secure, harness to cable, and the ride was a one-way express toward the ladder at the foot of the bridge.

Thrown helpless by the seas pouring by, her safety line humming like a harp string, she opened her eyes and looked forward. For one crazy moment she enjoyed the sight, the bow an express elevator up the side of a massive breaker curling as if to smother the ferret boat. Yet in a flash *Resolute* rode high above the seas, searchlight beams chalk white into the raging dark.

Chloe heard herself scream, half terror, half wild delight at the chaos ahead, until the bow dropped into the bottom of the next wave and a wall of foaming black toppled aft to crush her against the bulkhead. So this is their job, she thought, that dispassionate observer in her mind. I thought I knew them . . . I thought . . . even little Dhimine, she *asked* for this! *Who are these animals?*

Eyes wide, she leaped to the bridge ladder, her paws tight on the rails. The sea swept over her from head to tail, and she was surprised that it felt no colder than ice.

The instant the sea passed, she unsnapped her safety hook and bolted up the ladder to the bridge, wrenched the door open and hurled herself inside.

The captain turned, startled at the crash inside the bridge, saw the journalist gasp in the crimson glow of the night-lights.

"Clo! Hold tight!" Bethany spun the wheel to drive *Resolute* directly into the next sea, which would have tumbled the boat had it caught her broadside.

Glad to be alive, Chloe Ferret clung to the pawholds inside the bridge as the J-boat shuddered and righted, the wave sweeping over the ferret craft from deck to lookout stations. Through the armor glass she could see Harley's silhouette in the ruby glow of the Port High's night-lights, his muscled body braced against his harness, leaning into the storm as though he could sight the distress vessel by sheer force of will.

"I told you to get off the boat!" Bethany spun the wheel back to course, moving ahead wave by wave, turning directly into seas only when the safety of her ship depended on it. "I gave you an order!"

The rock star shivered. She couldn't remember the last time anyone had shouted at her. "I'm sorry, Captain! I was scared!"

"Stay right where you are, Chloe . . ." Bethany's voice was lost over the crash of the sea against the armor glass. ". . . not go back to your quarters, do not even move until we make it through . . ."

A crash of static, and Dhimine's voice came over the inter-phone and the bridge loudspeakers. "Starboard High has the vessel in sight, ma'am."

Stunned at the call, Bethany shot a glance to Dhimine's pelorus repeater. It was pointing nearly abeam on the starboard side. At the peak of the next wave, for just a moment, a radar return, some giant structure between her boat and the shore.

"Oh, come on!" she said. "Not possible!" But she knew it was. Without its rudder, *Deepsea Explorer* drifted broad abeam, its tall steel side to the storm, wind and sea push-ing it helpless toward Moray Reef.

"What's happened?" said Chloe.

Bethany spun the wheel hard to starboard, turning down-wind directly toward the ship. "She's going on the rocks, Clo."

The captain selected Rescue Frequency and pressed her microphone button. "Maytime Rescue," she called, "J-101 has the distress vessel in sight. She has broached to, point seven miles west of Moray Reef. We are commencing an upwind approach to the bow of the vessel, we have lights above."

Then to the interphone: "Port High, give us a flare, please, Harley."

A trail of sparks shot upward from the lookout station, turning the scene to daylight: the vast low bulk of *Deepsea Explorer* tilting downwind, seas bursting alongside, spray flying high over her decks.

"Attention, all paws," called Bethany. "This is a survivor rescue mission. We cannot save the distress vessel, she will be on the rocks within the hour. We are on a standard upwind approach to the bow section. All ahead one-third, please, Boa."

Below, the chief engine ferret reached his paw to the throttles and smoothly brought the power back to a steady purr. "Ahead one-third, aye."

"Highs," Bethany called, "give me searchlights astern, please."

Chloe glanced behind, caught her breath at the height of water rising there, threatening to engulf *Resolute* as the boat lost headway.

The captain struggled with the wheel, balancing them all on wind and wave. Even slowing, *Resolute* closed the distance to the giant hull in minutes. At close range Bethany could see the anchor chains from the hawseholes plunging straight down into the sea. The captain had tried to anchor, she thought, though the water offshore was too deep. The anchors wouldn't touch bottom until too late, until the vessel was over the shelf, and by then the ship would be lost.

"Bethany," said Chloe, "if the boat goes onshore, they'll be safe, won't they? I mean . . ."

The captain's voice came tonelessly, dispassionate, while her mind calculated wind and wave and distance. "No, Chloe. No, they will not be safe, they will be dead." She pressed the interphone button. "Sequential flares, please."

Just before Harley's flare was swallowed in the sea, Dhimine's was launched, a rocket trail upward, and daylight returned.

Looking astern over her shoulder in absolute concentration, picking the moment as one monster wave surged beneath them and before the next could rise, the captain turned the helm hard into the wind and *Resolute* spun like a weather vane seaward. "Stand by for ahead standard, Boa . . . stand by . . . *Now!*"

An instant calm response: "Ahead standard, aye."

Engines surging to halt her drift downwind, J-101 pressed ahead into the seas just enough to hold a position close to windward of *Deepsea Explorer*. In the giant ship's starboard hawsehole the captain saw two ship's rats, soaked in rain and seawater, waiting. Their lives depended now on *Resolute.*

"Dhimine, Harley, we'll need lines to the ship for the rescue cage. Lay them on the hawsehole, forward, by the sea rats. Take your time. Don't miss."

The captain looked ahead to the bow station, clenched her jaw. "Vink, I want you to take the cage up the lines as soon as they're fast."

Her brother's voice came back, expecting the order, no fear at what she had asked. "Cage is ready, ma'am. On your command . . ."

Dhimine fired her rescue line toward the stricken ship; an instant later Harley fired his to the same target.

The sea rats ducked inside the hawse tunnel as the lines shot toward them, but the second the ropes slapped home, they grabbed the ends and made them fast to the anchor chain.

Bethany pressed the interphone button. "Go, Vink!"

From the bridge, she watched her brother dash from his station with an awkward bundle of nylon web, snap his harness to the safety cable. Straightaway he was thrown by a sea bursting over the bows, tumbling him aft to the bridge. One paw clenched tight on the webbing, the other released the safety harness. Instantly the young ferret darted up the ladder to the Starboard High lookout station and reached for Dhimine's rescue line, stretched over the water to *Deepsea Explorer.*

The two sea rats cheered at the sight. "I told you they'd come!" shouted Jasper over the wind. "I *told* you the ferrets would come!"

Harley Ferret fired another parachute flare upwind, wishing it were he, not the ensign, taking the cage aboard. Yet he tended his duty, reloading the line launcher, setting another flare cartridge into its firing tube.

Cage slung like a backpack over his shoulders, the ensign darted out the rescue line toward *Deepsea Explorer*.

Harley watched, tense as iron, unsnapped his safety harness. If that animal goes into the water, he thought, I'm going after him.

Bethany didn't watch, intent on holding *Resolute* as steady as she could. Though they had practiced it over and again, running the cage in a force-eight gale was no easy task. One moment slack, the next hauling taut with a snap that would have hurled an untrained animal into the sea, the line was a living, writhing creature that did not allow a single misstep.

But like a circus ferret on the high wire, in the glare of searchlights and rocket flares, her brother darted ahead, stopped, darted ahead again, until he reached the hawsehole and the sea rats hauled him inside.

"Welcome to the ship," said Jasper to the dripping ferret. "How long do we have?"

Sammy looked at his friend, startled by the question.

"Maybe an hour, maybe not," said Vincent. "The anchor chains will slow us when they hit the shelf, but your ship's not going to make it." He brushed the water from his eyes with one soaking paw, unsnapped the rescue cage and assembled it, sliding the main pulley over one rescue line to *Resolute.* "How many animals aboard?"

"Over a hundred. They're most of 'em here," said the sea rat, turning to look down the hawse pipe, now a tunnel of frightened rodents. "Little guys first," he called. "Come on, you mice! Don't be afraid, it's the rescue ferrets!"

CHAPTER 9

"HELLO, *Resolute,* this is *Strongpaw.* We've got your lights in sight, we're taking station midships, with your permission."

The first cage of survivors loading, Bethany felt comfortable and in charge. A dangerous feeling, she knew, and summoned back anxiety. Complacency she would not allow.

"Welcome, *Strongpaw,* permission granted. We've got a cage on the line, we're taking off survivors forward. You might send a search team across, bring survivors up to the deck midships and run your cage from there. She'll be on the rocks before long."

"Aye, aye, Captain. What's your power to hold station?"

Bethany smiled in spite of herself. She was still unaccustomed to other commanders calling her *Captain*. "Ahead standard is working for us, Chet. It's a bit of a breeze out there."

"Busy night, hey?"

Bethany clicked her microphone button twice to agree.

On the bridge, Chloe Ferret seethed at her own inactivity. "I've got to do something, Bethany! Let me do something to help!"

The captain had every right to lock her below; any help the journalist knew how to give would only put her in harm's way. To lose the rock star at sea, for some, would be a greater disaster than losing *Deepsea Explorer*. Still, Chloe had trained earnestly with her crew, the captain thought, she was no cream puff. . . .

Now the first cage of survivors was on its way, twenty mice peering down in terror at the sea a-rage beneath them.

"You can help, Clo."

Chloe turned, watched her friend. "Tell me what I can do. Anything!"

"Harley's going to open the cage at the main companionway. The survivors won't know what to do or where to go. They'll be awfully scared. Meet them at the ladder belowdecks, tell them they're safe, take them to the survivors' quarters, put them in rescue blankets and hammocks. That'll help a lot!"

"Aye, aye, ma'am." She moved at once to the door, filled with purpose.

"*Your safety harness, Clo!* Keep your harness on, keep your harness snapped to that cable until you are belowdecks!"

"Aye, aye, Cap'n!"

Bethany shook her head. I must be crazy, she thought. But her order had been given. No sooner was her celebrity friend out the doorway than another towering sea thundered aboard, washing the decks shoulder high. Her paws torn from the cable by the force of it, Chloe was swept helplessly away for the length of her safety line, smashed to a wrenching stop. Drenched in seawater, the animal found her footing the second the sea was gone, darted to the main companionway, unsnapped her safety line and disappeared below.

The captain breathed a sigh of relief.

Topside, the cage and its survivors settled on deck, where Harley stood, securely fastened to his own safety cable.

Between waves he dragged the cage to the companionway, opened the webbing and cascaded the rodents below.

For a flash he caught Chloe's eyes as she waited, tossed her a salute. "First of your guests, ma'am!" he shouted.

She smiled to him and saluted back, in what he found a most attractive way. Then the door slammed shut and he was signaling Vincent to haul the empty webbing back to *Explorer*.

☁

The Coast Guard arrived in their massive cutter, secured rescue lines to the stern of the vessel and with the same practiced efficiency as the sea ferrets, began taking human survivors from the stricken ship. Before long, almost uneventfully, all were aboard, and the cutter cast off for home, shuttering a searchlight "Good luck" to the ferret J-boats.

For this they pay me, thought Bethany, taking a split second to enjoy the challenge and the danger of her job. Then she was back to work, the last of the mice, the parrot, the Sheltie and a stoic dripping calico cat in the next cage sliding down to *Resolute*. Only the ship's rats were still aboard, trusting the ferrets to lift them off.

Deepsea Explorer was sluggish and heavy now in the water, filling from the ragged hole that had been her starboard propeller-shaft tunnel and the seams that had failed forward. The more water poured inside, the faster the ship sank. The captain knew that she would not have much longer to bring aboard those brave rats.

Belowdecks, Chloe was an angel of calm for the survivors. Everywhere at once, she opened the bright yellow and orange rescue blankets, strung hammocks for the exhausted mice, comforted as best she could.

One mouse, mahogany brown with a blaze of white at her nose and chest, cried inconsolably, "They're gone, they're gone!"

Chloe tucked the blanket tighter around its shoulders. "The ship is lost," she soothed, "but you're safe, and your friends. Ships can be replaced."

"You don't understand," said the mouse. "The disks! Everything we went to find, everything we learned, it's all on board, it'll go down with the ship!"

"There will be other voyages," said Chloe, kneeling at her side.

"No! From all the data we gathered, we thought it was too late, we thought it was the end, *but we found how to reverse it!* The ocean does not have to die! It's all in the disks and the disks are going down!"

Ever so slightly, Bethany Ferret relaxed. There's time, she thought, there's time and a little to spare, to get all off.

Each storm has a personality, and in the course of the rescue *Resolute*'s captain had come to know the ways of this one. Turning the helm to let the wind take her boat backward, just a little, when the line went tight, then straight again into the seas to gain headway before it sagged. She found the rhythms of its waves and its cross-swells, learned with practice just how to counter the force of the gale, hold the cage line nearly steady against the wind and all but the most powerful seas. With those, the line dipped to the water or whipped tight as iron, no matter what she did with rudder or engine.

Her paws easy on the helm, she watched the last cage of survivors slide down the rescue line. The mission was nearly finished.

Then she saw something that she could barely believe. She whipped her head so fast that her rescue cap fell to the deck of the bridge. She saw a blur against the storm: there was an animal climbing the ladder to Starboard High, there was Chloe Ferret, grasping the rescue line and running, four paws top speed, no safety cable, above the knife-edge seas to the hulk of the near-sunken ship.

"CHLOE!"

Bethany pressed the interphone button. *"Starboard High, report to the bridge now! Dhimine, you have command of the boat!"*

There was a startled squeak in response, but immediately the littlest ferret dropped from her station to the bridge companionway, raced up the ladder.

Harley, waiting on deck for the cage, looked up, thunderstruck, saw the rock star on the high rope. Only years of Rescue Service discipline kept him from following her at once. There were survivors in the cage, and they'd be swept away if he did not take them below.

The lean young ferret leaped into the air a second before the cage arrived on deck, caught it and shoved it forward to the companionway, dumped the animals below and shut the door tight.

Harley looked to the bridge at the instant its door slammed open, saw Dhimine take the helm, watched Bethany fly in one bound to the deck, another to the Starboard High lookout ladder, then out the rescue line after Chloe Ferret.

Vincent met his sister at the hawsehole, astonished that she would leave the bridge in the midst of . . .

"Where'd she go, Vink?"

"The computer room aft!" her brother told her. "Said she had to get the data! What data? Why—"

"Clo's gone crazy!" said the captain. "Get back to the boat, I'll find her and drag her out!"

"Bethany, let me get her."

"No! She's my responsibility! Go, Vink! That is an order!"

He stiffened. "Aye, aye, ma'am!"

"And stand by to take us aboard before this thing goes down!" She cuffed him gently with her paw, then disappeared aft at a run.

Her brother snapped his safety harness to the lifeline, stepped out of the hawsehole and ran down the slope of the rescue line toward *Resolute*. At that moment, though, a giant sea lifted *Resolute* like a toy, the rope went bar-tight, spray flying from the fibers, then it snapped and Ensign Vincent Ferret tumbled headlong into the sea.

At once he inflated his life vest, at once his strobe light began flashing, but he was adrift in the very waves that pounded the humans' ship toward the rocks. The tiny, tenth-of-a-second flash of his light fired more often than not underwater, hidden by the fury of the storm.

For Harley Ferret, it all happened softly. He watched Vincent begin his run down the rescue line as though in some terrible slow-honey nightmare, watched the line stretch and part, watched his friend tumble dreamlike through the air—a colored pinwheel of scarf and life vest and sable fur—and fall, ever so slowly, into the sea.

Dhimine watched, too, from the bridge. Trembling uncontrollably, she saw Harley, no thought for his own life and apparently with no plan to return to *Resolute,* leap straightaway into the sea toward Vincent's beacon flash.

Just then *Strongpaw* slipped its lines and cleared the *Explorer.* "We've got 'em, *Resolute*! We've run a Lost Mouse, there are no animals belowdecks. Take it easy going back, hey?"

Dhimine did not hear. She touched the interphone button, amazed at how cool her voice sounded from the captain's station, no matter how her paws and body shook. "Boa, engines ahead one-third and on deck now! Vincent's in the water, Harley's overboard after him. Get to Starboard High and lay a line on them now, please!"

She planned to drift backward toward the hulk, saving distance for the rescue, though it brought *Resolute* perilously close to the iron cliff of the vessel. She trusted Boa to find the two in the water, to fire a rescue line as accurately in wind and sea as she could do it herself. If the line did not touch the ferrets in the water, if it did not wrap itself around them, they'd have no way of knowing it had even been fired. They'd be gone.

The best she could do for now was to steer the boat, and that is what she did.

Increasing pressure belowdecks detonated *Deepsea Explorer*'s forward hatch cover away as though by dynamite, seas flooding in, and still Dhimine held *Resolute* directly into the storm. She could hope to rescue Vincent and Harley; she had no idea what had happened to Chloe and the captain.

CHAPTER 10

Bᴇᴛʜᴀɴʏ Fᴇʀʀᴇᴛ threw open the door to the computer data room, now barely above the waves thundering aboard, steadily swallowing *Deepsea Explorer* into the abyss off Moray Reef.

Burrowing behind the shelf of boxed computer disks, tumbling them to the deck, Chloe Ferret jumped down and began dragging the boxes into a large orange-colored bag, white letters: *Intership Delivery.*

"The mouse told me, Bethany! It's research! The animals, the oceans, the future, it took them years, they have the answer at last! It's all here! It can't go down with the boat!"

For an irrational second, the captain wanted to explain the difference between a boat and a ship. "We're sinking, Clo! When this thing goes under we're going with it unless we get off *now*!"

The other wasn't hearing. "Then get off, Bethany! I won't go unless the disks go with me!"

The captain grabbed the bag, dragged it to the disks, pushed sealed boxes inside with all paws. Blue plastic boxes, white labels: *Ozone Depletion and Recovery, Coral Regrowth Statistics, Ocean Temperature Soundings, Data Correlation Curves.*

"Chloe, I swear I am going to lock you below, I'm going to put you on ferret food and water, I'm going to hang your hat so high . . ."

CHAPTER 11

I N THE WATER, Harley found, it was not just difficult, it was impossible to see the flash of Vincent's rescue beacon. Now and then he thought he saw the dimmest of flickers, and he swam toward them. He trusted his life and the first officer's to Dhimine. Somehow he knew the little ferret would . . . somehow, she would find them before the giant alongside went to the bottom.

He heard Vincent's voice, faintly over the roar of water. *"HARLEY! DON'T . . . YOU CAN'T BE HERE . . . GET BACK TO THE BOAT!"*

A dim, wet flash, not five paws away, the glow of a colored scarf in the flarelight.

"AYE, AYE, SIR!" he shouted. *"LET'S BOTH OF US . . . BACK TO THE BOAT, SIR!"*

Drifting astern at low power, the seas still raked *Resolute*'s deck. On Dhimine's command, Boa clambered from below to the main deck, then up the ladder directly to the Starboard High lookout station. He saw nothing in the water between *Resolute* and the sinking hulk. Nothing but seas, their tops blown away like shrapnel in the gale.

The chief engine ferret grabbed binoculars in the very moment the parachute flare sank to the water and went out; the world turned to black, split only by *Resolute*'s twin searchlights. Then, outside the shafts of those lights, came a tiny flash in the ebony sea. Another flash, alongside the first, swept by currents away from the ferret vessel.

Boa's huge paw grasped the rescue-line gun, spun it aft on its pivot. He judged the wind, aimed to windward of the twin sparkles in the dark, squeezed the trigger.

At once, he reached to the flare launcher, hoping it was loaded, and fired. Sparks shot up, the darkest of pauses, then noon hung once again over the site. He followed the lay of the line on the water, saw two yellow life jackets directly down the center of the line.

"Yes!" he shouted in the storm. *"Got 'em both!"* Now you guys hang on, he thought. All you have to do is hang on and Boa's gonna haul you in.

Awash in the seas, the black iron of *Deepsea Explorer* had become a reef itself, as dangerous as any rocks ashore. *Resolute,* drifting backward, was two giant waves from tearing her propellers against the wreck. It was all Dhimine could do to steer the boat, and the moment Boa had fired the lifeline she pressed the interphone. "All ahead two-thirds, Boa! We're drifting into the ship!"

The big ferret tumbled down the ladder from the lookout station, no safety harness. A wave swept aboard as his paws touched the deck, and only his great weight kept him upright. He staggered in the surge, then threw himself at the engine-room companionway, caught the rail with one paw, wrenched the door open, dropped down the ladder. Before he recovered his balance from the drop, he pushed both throttles forward.

His interphone headset lay on the deck, but he spoke aloud nevertheless. "Ahead two-thirds, aye!"

White water burst from the propellers, a few paws from the steel that would bend them useless.

Love you! Boa thought to his engines. Never did he doubt that they would answer their throttles.

On the bridge, Dhimine held her breath and watched while *Resolute* crept away from the black steel.

Boa heaved himself up the ladder to the rescue line. He wrapped it about his massive paws and hauled. It felt in the storm and seas as though the line were fast to the wreck itself.

"Ha-ha!" he shouted, an animal gone mad in the tempest. *"Gotcha both!"*

The big ferret hauled as he never had in his life, lower paws braced against *Resolute*'s stern rail, the steel bending ever so slightly. He growled, powerful shoulders trembling, pulling in the rescue line, paw over paw, the storm raging seas against him, from time to time swirling him out of sight in black water.

"No, you don't!" he snarled, teeth clenched, into the fury. *"Nobody takes these animals from Boa!"*

CHAPTER 12

Between the two of them, Bethany and Chloe stuffed the orange bag half-full of computer disks, all the boxes from the shelf marked *Expedition Records.* Chloe threw three lightning half-hitches around the throat of the bag, the extra one for luck, snapped a bowline on the end for a handle.

"Let's take more!" she said, reaching for another bag. "Just in case. *Expedition Video* sounds important!"

"No!" shouted Bethany. She felt the ship groan under-paw, giant pressures building within as it settled. *"Chloe, no! No! No!"*

The two animals dragged the bag from the computer room onto the bridge, a task made easier now by deeper water over the deck—the bag floated more than it dragged.

They splashed toward the bridge railing in the instant the midships hatch cover exploded in a fountain of salt spray, the sound of near-miss dynamite.

Seconds, thought Bethany. We have seconds before she goes down. Chloe pulled for the windward side, till the captain shouted, "Lee side! *Lee side!*"

Chloe was not certain which was the lee side, then remembered. Of course, she thought. The water's too wild to windward, we'd be gone.

At once she turned back toward Bethany. The sight would stay with her for the rest of her life: the trim officer sil-houetted in the stark light of a parachute flare, the whole scene in blacks and whites, save for that cherry-lemon scarf proud at her throat.

Too late, Bethany thought. Looking into the storm, even Chloe knew they were doomed. There was no time for fear, no time for regrets.

Abruptly, faster than the ferret officer thought possible, *Deepsea Explorer* sank. One second the forward half of the ship was awash, the next it was gone in foam and spray, the ship turning nearly straight down, the deck under the two animals suddenly became a wall down which they slid, dropping heavily onto the bridge railing now a floor over the abyss, the entire vessel lifting, then dropping like stone into the sea.

"Hang on, Clo!" Bethany shouted, though she knew nothing could help them now. Whether they hung on or let go, the great ship would drag them under; either *Explorer* would take them, or the whirlpools that would follow her to the bottom.

In that moment the lieutenant felt a strange and perfect peace. Nothing else mattered. Not the data, not the storm, not their adventure on this minor planet of a minor sun in a minor galaxy of stars flung across space and time. Everything was just as it should be. She was about to give her life that others would live, and it was proper that she should. It was as though the storm had ended, the wind and seas turned calm.

She smiled at her friend. "Take my paw, Clo."

Chloe, feeling the same lovely peace, reached her paw to her friend's. "It's all right, isn't it, Bethany?" she said quietly. The black hull slipped down.

In that peace, a broad, warm light spread across the sea. An arc of color, a giant rainbow, shimmered about them, lofting up, perfect gentle lights, away into the sky.

Before them, as softly as though they had simply not noticed, stood a small, sable-color ferret, looking upon them with the most exquisite knowing love. Every shred of fear and doubt vanished in the presence of this creature.

"Bethany," it said, a voice they heard in their mind more than in their ears. "Chloe."

Then it was silent for a time that could have been an age. They beheld that creature uncaring of time. In that forever-second, the two of them remembered who they were, where they had come from, why they had wanted these life-times on earth.

Of course, thought Bethany. How could I have forgotten? So much she yearned to go with the lovely animal, how ready she was to follow wherever it might show the way to walk.

"This is not your time to cross the bridge," said the ferret. "You have much yet to learn and to do in the places and times you have chosen to express yourselves, you have many adventures ahead." The two ferrets looked into those dark eyes, unable to move or speak. "You've followed your highest sense of right, so far, through all your tests. Well done."

The creature came near, lifted its paw, touched their shoulders. "Here's the reminder you wished." It looked deep into Chloe's eyes. "Express beauty."

Slowly, evenly, it turned to gaze upon Bethany. "Express love."

It stayed with them, timeless, surrounding them with joy.

Then it slipped away, dissolving into a place more real than the ferrets' here and now, and was gone. Gone, too, the arc of color, the light fading away.

Standing together, swept in happiness, the two animals were all at once knocked from their paws by a bone-jarring, dragging thunder. In a flash the storm raged around them as it had before, seas breaking and churning below.

Instead of sinking, *Deepsea Explorer* shuddered to rest at an angle nearly vertical, her anchors and chains into the abyss, her bow stuck fast on the granite shelf.

Bethany blinked. They had just been given the minutes they needed to live.

"Now, Clo!"

The ferrets dragged the bag between them to the railing's end, overlooking a lake of calm protected from storm by the hulk of *Deepsea Explorer*.

The ship was lost, Bethany knew, but with the bow stuck on the rocks below, it would take a few seconds longer for the stern to follow. There would be suctions and down-currents, but death was no longer certain.

"Jump!"

They threw the bag overboard and followed it into the dark, into the water between the wreck and the breakers downwind.

Their life-jacket beacons flashed, bright and clear in the smooth icy water.

"Swim, Clo! Away from the wreck!" It had been drilled into the rescue ferret: never let it happen, survivors in the water near a ship going down.

Like two sudden otters, the ferrets swam as hard as they could, towing the bag behind them.

"Bethany . . ." her voice faded.

"Are you all right, Clo?"

"Did you see . . . ?"

"Later, Clo! We'll think about it later!" said the sea ferret. "Now we swim!"

Then the sky broke open over them in a blaze of light. Slicing like an arrow across the calm water came *Resolute* and her glare of searchlights, turning hard to port, sliding broadside to halt ahead of the two animals in the water.

Harley Ferret didn't stop with the boat. He flew over the side, together with Ensign Vincent Ferret, diving to his sister.

"Get aboard!" shouted Bethany to her brother as he surfaced, frightened they could all be lost in the currents. "I can swim faster than you can!"

Vincent reached a paw to the bag of disks. "Then I'll race you, Sis."

Chloe called from the dark, "Harley!"

By then the lean ferret was at her side, his paw reaching for hers. "You're safe, Miss Chloe," he said. "We're almost there."

From deck, Boa reached down and hauled the animals from the water two at a time in his great paws, first the captain and her brother, then the rock star and her rescuer.

There came a last explosion from the hulk, the stern hatch blowing away from pressures it could no longer resist. The towering steel mass groaned in the night, leaned ponderously toward the ferret rescue boat.

Boa shouted to the bridge, Harley and Chloe still hanging from his arms as the hulk grew over them, toppling down in slow motion. "Got 'em, Dhimine! *Get us out of here!*"

"Power, Boa! I need all ahead flank!"

In a miracle, before the chief could move, *Resolute*'s engines burst into life, cracking full-throttle thunders. Dhimine was nearly yanked off her paws by the acceleration, but she steered the boat, raced it from beneath the falling disaster and back into the storm.

"Ahead standard!" she called as *Resolute* struck the first of the wild seas once again.

A monster fountain of flying water, and *Deepsea Explorer* went down, in her place a vast slick of violent suctions and whirlpools. The storm swept in, raging to the rocks as though the giant had never floated there.

"Ahead standard, aye," said Bethany from the engine room, the throttles under her paws. "Good save, Captain!"

Trembling, the little ferret at the helm touched the interphone button. "Thank you, ma'am," she said, flooded in relief, turning *Resolute* head-on into the seas.

Harley Ferret saw Chloe safely belowdecks, then scrambled aloft to Port High.

114

Bethany turned the engine room back to Boa, climbed the ladder to the bridge, opened the door.

Dhimine saluted, relinquishing the helm. "Your boat, Captain."

Bethany touched her paw to her brow. "Thank you, Dhimine. Give me a station check when you can, please."

With a nod the exhausted little ferret was out the door and up the ladder to her post.

Then came her voice on the interphone: "Starboard High, main searchlight, on. Secondary is on . . . and off. Smoke flares, parachute flares . . ."

"All searchlights off," called the captain when the checks were finished. "Look sharp for the Maytime jetty light!"

Resolute plunged through the seas on her return a little more slowly, a little less violently than she had on her race to the disaster. The captain steered well to windward of the jetty, those dark rocks waiting in the night.

"All lookouts," she called, "I have intermittent radar on the buoy, no returns from the jetty." Odd, she thought. The radar reflectors on the jetty carried away? Careful, Bethany!

Now the screen showed a clear return from the radar buoy. It was safe to turn, whether she could see or not, into the channel to her left.

"Breakers on the port side!" called Harley, and at once his searchlight stabbed into the black.

At the limit of the light, through the swirling veils of seawater, Bethany saw the faint surging glow of seas on rocks.

"Not again!" she said aloud. *"Be careful, Captain!"*

The radar buoy, chained to its concrete block at the bottom of the channel, had once more been dragged from its position in a storm. A shock of cold went through her.

"All stations," she called, "the buoy's dragged! We need a visual on the jetties!"

For a long minute there was silence on the interphone, night-vision binoculars from three stations straining for some glimpse . . .

"The port-side jetty's in sight," came Vincent's voice, calm and even. The center pelorus repeater above Bethany's armor glass swung thirty degrees to port, the forward searchlight flashing out, catching a single red reflector set above the rocks.

Came Harley's voice: "Port High's got the jetty."

"Starboard High's got the starboard jetty," called Dhimine. Her searchlight caught a green reflector through the storm, held it fast.

Bethany guided *Resolute* carefully downwind, the vessel feeling its way on the beams of its searchlights like some seagoing rock climber through a wind-whipped crevasse. Heavy rollers swept between the jetties, smothering the rocks in foam, last chance to crush J-101 as they had before.

That will not be, thought Bethany, her paws firmly on the helm, her rescue cap pushed to the back of her head. *That will not be!*

CHAPTER 13

D OCKSIDE, all survivors stayed for a while on deck, the mice nearly invisible under their bright FRS rescue blankets. "Of course you can keep the blankets," Chloe told each one. "Take them home, courtesy of the Ferret Rescue Service!"

The gifts were unauthorized, Bethany later explained to the base commander, though it might be a thoughtful policy to consider for the future.

Then the bedraggled creatures shuttled off in buses to hot meals and warm beds. *Deepsea Explorer*'s computer disks, neatly boxed, were driven away in a van to the Maytime Coast Guard station.

As her crew secured *Resolute* after the mission, Bethany touched the button for the ship's speakers. "Attention, all paws."

They stopped and listened from on deck and belowdecks, swells rocking the boat even in its berth.

"I cannot tell you," came the captain's voice, "how proud I am . . . how proud *Resolute* must be, of her crew this night." She took the rescue cap from her head, wiped tears away, unashamed.

Rain pelted down as they listened in silence.

"Well done, Boa."

The big ferret stood in the engine room, a rag in his paw. He had been wiping down his gleaming diesels, thanking them for the work they had done. She's a good captain, he thought.

"Well done, Harley."

Doin' my job, Skipper, he thought, just doin' my job.

"Well done, Dhimine."

The littlest ferret shook her head. If you only knew how frightened I was . . .

"Well done, Vink."

He nodded, at his station. Mom's proud of you, Sis.

"And you, Chloe . . . well done!"

In the survivors' quarters, folding hammocks and returning them to lockers, the rock star felt sudden, hot tears in her eyes. She had come for a story. How much more she had found!

"With the crew's permission, from all of us . . ." Bethany's voice echoed across J-101, and through the rain-slick docks. "Well done, *Resolute*. You saved lives. Theirs and ours."

The captain put down the microphone and let relief wash over her. Alone on the bridge, she sobbed as though her heart would break, as though it could not contain the love she felt for all ferrets, for all the animals she had ever known.

CHAPTER 14

FOR TWO DAYS the storm raged on, till finally the third dawned in sunlight and a breezy, blue sky. At noon, Chloe's silver limousine whispered to a stop alongside *Resolute*'s berth. The driver, impeccably groomed, waited patiently at the rear door.

Bethany stood by the helm, Harley curled on the storm-shield above the Port High lookout, the two ferrets working to install a night-vision repeater link to the bridge.

"I'm getting hash on the screen, Harley. We've got a loose connection. "

Looking up, the captain saw Chloe emerge from belowdecks, carrying her notebooks. She walked slowly, thoughtfully, toward the bridge, touching good-bye to J-101's familiar pawrails and safety cables.

"Stand by, Harley," said Bethany.

She heard the knock on the bridge entry door. "Come in, Clo."

There were tears in the rock star's eyes. "I'm going back, Bethany, and I don't want to go!"

The officer hugged her friend. "Some of us serve on boats, Clo, some of us don't. Some behind the spotlights, some in front." Bethany watched the lovely ferret's eyes. "That doesn't matter. *Express beauty* does."

Chloe blinked, startled. "You saw it! The most beautiful, loving . . . it wasn't a dream?"

"Maybe. But I'll never forget." There was a long silence, the two remembering. "And the Rainbow Bridge, we dreamed that together."

"No!" said Chloe. "You and me, we weren't asleep!" She was still for a time, then brushed her eye with her paw. "I saw it." She turned to Bethany, her voice a whisper. "My mother said I would, someday, when my life was done."

Bethany nodded. "Mine, too."

Katrinka Ferret hadn't been dreaming when she died. She had told her eldest kit what she saw as she saw it, and she had been filled with joy. What Bethany remembered most about that night was how happy her mother had been, the dazzling colors of love that had filled the room.

The Rainbow Bridge may not be of this world, Bethany thought, but it's somewhere, waiting. It's real.

The two talked for a while about what had happened, what they had seen at the railing of *Deepsea Explorer,* how they had changed because of it. Near-death vision of the ferrets' way to heaven or a gentle hallucination they had shared, they would tell no other animal of that scene for years to come.

In time, the captain touched the loudspeaker button. "All paws on deck midships," she said quietly into the microphone, and followed her friend down the bridge ladder to the main deck.

Chloe Ferret was surrounded by a family she had not known, joined in their promise to risk their lives to save animals from harm.

"We know you have to go," said Bethany. "We wish you didn't. You'll always be part of *Resolute.*"

Harley nodded, a bold smile. "You can sing for me anytime, Clo. Anytime you want."

The rock star embraced him, rubbed his muscled back. "Dear brave Harley," she whispered, "I'll always sing for you."

The littlest ferret, down from her station and smelling of brass polish, hid her face in her paws, her hat askew. "Oh, Clo . . ."

"Hey, Dhimine," Chloe whispered through her tears, embracing the sea ferret who seemed no older than a kit. "Chin up. Friends forever, okay?"

The lookout nodded bravely.

"You'd best remember your knots," said Boa gruff big oil-stained creature. "They'll save your life, you know, someday. They could."

Chloe declined to shake his paw, chose a hug in which she nearly disappeared from sight. "I'll not forget!"

"There's my shipmate," he said, releasing her.

Before she quite left his embrace, she kissed his cheek, surprised them both. "Write to me, Boa!"

126

The first officer stood nearby. "A privilege to sail with you, Miss Chloe."

"Oh, Vincent!" She shook her head at his formality, hugging him till he laughed and backed away.

At the gangway, she paused, turned to face the flag of the FRS. "If I hadn't lost my hat, I'd salute the ship."

"You didn't lose your hat, Clo," said the captain, "you found it."

Bethany lifted her battered rescue-cap and placed it on the star's sleek head. Then she slipped the knot of her cherry-lemon crew-scarf and drew it around the neck of her friend. "You are loved."

Chloe Ferret's eyes filled once again with tears. She stood erect and saluted the ship's pennant, torn and frayed, fluttering from its halyard aloft. Then she ducked into her limousine and the driver shut the door.

Resolute's crew watched the wave of her paw behind charcoal glass, and she was gone.

"That," said Bethany, "is one beautiful ferret."

"Aye, aye," said her crew quietly.

The captain straightened, took control of her feelings. "I believe we have a practice at fifteen thirty hours," she said briskly. "We stand alert tomorrow from oh six hundred hours. Everybody ready?"

"I miss her," said Dhimine.

Boa patted her shoulder. "We all do."

Bethany squared her shoulders. "I doubt that's the last we'll see of Chloe Ferret," she said. "She's got work to do, and so do we. Harley, I'd like to finish the night cam before practice."

CHAPTER 15

Rescues come in threes, the sea ferrets believed, and it was so. The first day *Resolute* stood alert after the *Deepsea Explorer* storm, the siren went off for the trawler *Libby J. Haines,* capsized from overload.

She was keel-up when they arrived, the ship turned lifeboat for the human crew and a dozen shivering mice. *Mild seas, easy rescue,* wrote Bethany in the ship's log. *Twelve lives.*

So it went, from rescue to rescue. Hours and hours of boredom, they say in the FRS, punctuated by moments of stark terror. Yet that was the life that each of them had chosen, and not one would trade it for another.

In July, Chloe's story made the cover of *Mustelid* magazine, a striking sunset photo of *Resolute* off the Maytime jetties, flying seaward in a cloud of golden spray, her lookouts silhouetted at their posts, her skipper on the bridge, wearing the sky like a scarf.

Copies were everywhere: in offices on the Maytime station, in crews' quarters, even in the mess hall, open on the dining tables. Sea and shore ferrets alike read and stared, finding their own image now and then in the photo backgrounds. They thrust pens and magazines at Bethany and her crew for autographs.

In August the posters went up for the rock concert, *Zsa-Zsa and the Show Ferrets,* in benefit for the Ferret Rescue Service at Maytime.

A day before the event, the three stars arrived at the dock in a white limousine, Chloe wearing her battered rescue-cap and crew-scarf, Zsa-Zsa and Mistinguette in large dark sunglasses. For the afternoon they met and talked with the rescue ferrets, toured *Resolute.* Chloe showed Boa that she could still tie a bowline with the snap of her paw, at least on the second attempt, and no one thought it strange that the two talked privately for quite some time.

The visitors crowded onto the bridge for a practice run during which Dhimine found the Lost Mouse in just under forty seconds.

What happened at the concert is not part of this tale, though it must be said that Zsa-Zsa opened with "Wild Ferret." The three performed "Just Close Your Eyes" as purely as ever they had, and their friend Whitepaw appeared from a blast of smoke and flame to join "If I Could Fly," a number that brought every ferret in the audience to its paws in delight.

At the end of the evening, Chloe took the stage in her *Resolute* scarf and cap, Misty and Zsa-Zsa backing her so gently on "Night Rescue" that there were tears in all their eyes before the last chord haunted into silence and the lights cut to black.

An hour after the concert the Show Ferrets were still swamped by autograph seekers, unwilling to break away from the animals they had charmed.

Yet this time the crew of *Resolute* blinked as long into flash cameras as the rock stars, signed their names for fans awed by the presence of real-life rescue ferrets, close enough to touch.

In the midst of pandemonium, Dhimine looked up, suddenly realizing, to Bethany.

"Captain," she asked, "are we famous?"

The words were caught in a firework of photoflash, and her picture appeared on the cover of *Celebrity Ferrets,* her question turned large type below.

CHAPTER 16

CELEBRITY FADES, character doesn't.

Bethany and Vincent, Boa and Harley and Dhimine and the J-boat crews of Ferret Rescue Station Maytime are no longer in the spotlights. They are still behind them, however, still on duty at the edge of the sea.

Not long after the *Deepsea Explorer* rescue, Dhimine applied for Sea Ferret Officers' School, and on her service record and the recommendations of her captain and the Maytime base commander, she was accepted.

The competition for Dhimine's position at *Resolute*'s Starboard High lookout was intense. In one afternoon Bethany had fourteen interviews from highly qualified applicants.

The last was her second meeting with one Kimiko Ferret, who had impressed Bethany not so much by her lofty marks in training as by what seemed to be an inborn knowledge of J-boats and by a certain awareness of her mission, a quality Bethany sensed more than saw.

The young animal came from a family of sea ferrets and watched the captain with absolute confidence at the end of the interview. "I promise you, ma'am," she said, "that you have found the best lookout in the service, save for one since promoted."

"Save for one?"

"Do I look familiar to you, ma'am? Have you seen me before?"

"I expect I have," said Bethany, "or you wouldn't have asked."

The sea ferret's gaze never wavered. "Don't you remember, Captain? Survivor number eight? You came back down the line and found me in the sail locker."

Where do these animals come from? her friend Chloe once had asked. Now Bethany accepted a fact, no more questions. We come for love, we come for beauty, we come because it is our destiny to serve.

"So you're back," she said to the youngster. She watched her applicant for a long moment, and at last she shook her head. "The best save one, Kimiko? No. I need the best sea ferrets on my boat, the best but none, and I'll have nothing less." Bethany stood. The interview was over.

The applicant rose at once. "Yes, ma'am. Thank you, ma'am!"

So confident, Bethany thought. "We launch at dawn. We'll use no radar. Distress ship unknown, position unknown. I'll expect you on duty at Starboard High, and I'll expect you to sight the vessel first."

"I will, ma'am!"

As the sea ferret saluted and turned to leave, the captain saw herself in the young animal, she saw Dhimine and Harley and Vincent and Boa, she saw the spirit of all the rescue ferrets at Maytime.

"A minute," she said.

"Yes, ma'am?"

On the captain's desk lay a narrow wooden box. She opened it, drew forth a long fold of silk, bright angled stripes of cherry-lemon. She slipped it about Kimiko's neck, fastened it with a square knot.

"From your boat," she said, "from *Resolute*. Welcome aboard."

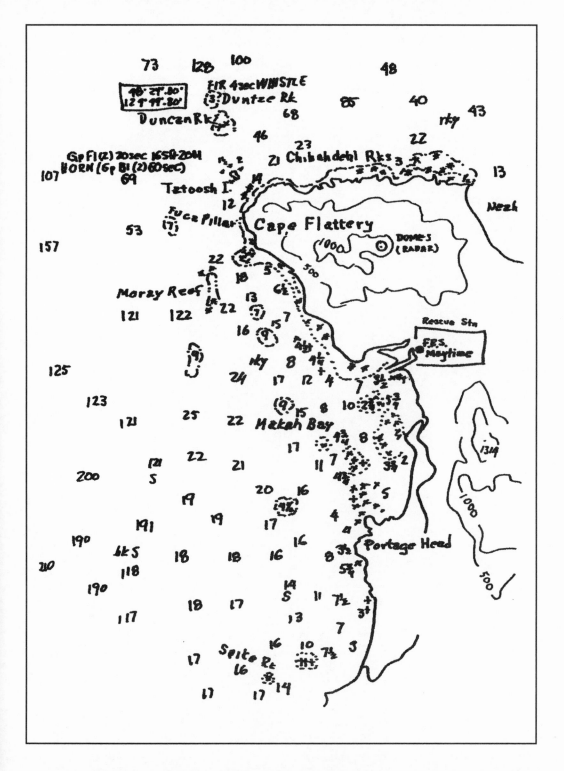